A True Likeness

An Austen Ensemble, Book 2

Corrie Garrett

Kindle Direct Publishing
LOS ANGELES, CALIFORNIA

Corrie Garrett
10424 Clybourn Ave.
Sunland, CA 91040
www.corriegarrett.wordpress.com

Publisher's Note: This is a work of fiction. Names, characters, places, and incidents are a product of the author's imagination. Locales and public names are sometimes used for atmospheric purposes. Any resemblance to actual people, living or dead, or to businesses, companies, events, institutions, or locales is completely coincidental.

Book Layout ©2017 BookDesignTemplates.com

A True Likeness/ Corrie Garrett. -- 1st ed.
ISBN 978-1-6791267-2-7

To my sister Elisabeth, a mother, painter, and artist, who made writing a portraitist far less intimidating.

"I wish nature had made such hearts as yours more common."

–JANE AUSTEN, PERSUASION

DEAR GEORGIANA,

Your brother insists on calling me Elizabeth rather than Lizzy. I do not at all mind, but has he always struggled with nicknames? Were you ever Georgie or Anna or some other pet name?

I am trying to gauge the depth of his formality, you see, the scope of the excavation I have taken on. Sometimes I do not know how to go on with him! It is rather like using the finest china every day. How does one relax?

It is very formidable to be always Elizabeth, and the soon-to-be Elizabeth Darcy is even more austere. I am not at all sure that Elizabeth Darcy would be impertinent or unconventional, which Lizzy too often is!

But enough of that, you asked after my sisters, and I can only say that they are well, but each is well according to her nature. Jane is in such transports of happiness that were our entire home to be washed away in a flood—it is *such a rainy summer!—she would find something good to say of it.*

Mary has discovered a new interest in a book of Christian martyrs and is always ready with a cheerful anecdote of dismemberment or raging beasts when we run out of topics during our wedding visits.

And Kitty is at last reconciled to staying home this summer because of the wedding. She has even ceased to long for Brighton and the officers more than once a day. My youngest sister, Lydia, is still visiting there, you see, and that has been a sad blow to Kitty's fortitude.

Jane and I have decided on a joint wedding day, with Mr. Bingley's and your brother's approval. I don't think my mother loves the idea of forgoing two wedding feasts for one, but we brought her around by pointing out that the novelty would make it the talk of Hertfordshire for at least a twelvemonth.

And how are you faring at Rosings? I regret that our engagement should have driven a (hopefully temporary) rift between Mr. Darcy and Lady Catherine. I am still full of admiration and a certain amount of guilt that you have thrown yourself into the breach. Remember that reinforcements are but a letter away. Merely ask and I know your brother will be there directly!

Yours,

Lizzy

A True Likeness

Georgiana tiptoed quietly into the library, where her cousin Anne was sitting for a portrait. The thick floral carpet helped muffle her footsteps, but still somehow the portraitist sensed her approach, throwing a quick look and greeting in her direction.

"Good afternoon, Miss Darcy."

His easel was set up about three yards from Anne's position just next to the glass doors of the terrace. The heavy mahogany desk which had formerly occupied that spot had been removed by three footmen and the butler to the other side of the library, where it blocked at least four tiers of shelved books. In its place had been put a graceful chintz lounge, Anne's seat for the portrait. Heavy, spattered drop cloths protected the area around the easel, and a strong smell of turpentine and oil pervaded the room.

On the wall behind Anne's position was the de Bourgh coat of arms, carefully positioned for the portrait. Through the doors could be seen the low, graceful pillars that surrounded the terrace, a bit of the fields beyond, and the sky. Today it was cloudy and gray, a dark day for June, but in the painting, diffuse sunlight seemed to spill into the room both from the door and from the viewer's left side. It was not quite the moody lighting of the romantics, but Georgiana secretly thought it was beautiful.

Mrs. Annesley, Georgiana's own companion, crocheted near the fireplace, which was lit for warmth. Georgiana drifted toward her and warmed her cold hands by the fire.

Today Mr. Turner would continue putting Anne into the beautifully painted background. At least, that was what Georgiana thought he planned to do during this sitting. Instead, he had set the canvas aside, and was sketching Anne's face on paper.

Anne was well-dressed, but her face held very little expression.

"It looks as if we might have a summer shower today," Mr. Turner said. "Will you drive out as usual, Miss de Bourgh?"

"Yes."

He began to darken the fold line above Anne's right eye, and Georgiana was drawn forward almost against her will. She didn't want to be a bother or a distraction, but she did find it so interesting to watch him draw.

"What do you think about when you drive?" he asked.

"I have never considered."

Mr. Turner's hand hesitated for the briefest moment around her mouth, but then he kept refining the sketch. "Do you prefer to take the same route every day, or do you enjoy variation?"

"Generally, the same. I drive by the parsonage and speak with Mr. or Mrs. Collins if they are at home. I circle to the north, around the village, and then back to Rosings." She said all this in a near monotone.

Mr. Turner's straight shoulders slumped slightly. "Thank you, Miss de Bourgh, that will be all for today. I have the positional sketch, but with the light so poor, I cannot do much more. Thank you for your time."

She rose and curtseyed properly. "Until dinner, Mr. Turner."

Mrs. Annesley began to pack up her yarn, and Mr. Turner, his pencils. He was a man of medium height, not much taller than Georgiana herself, and always dressed plainly, in dark colors.

"Were you trying to make her smile?" Georgiana asked.

He looked around at her. He was not handsome in the established way, but had a square, honest face, blue eyes, and hair between sand and brown that he kept unfashionably short. "Not necessarily smile," he said carefully. "The goal is to find something that brings out her personality, a look to capture, an intensity, but... She is very self-controlled."

Georgiana knew exactly what he meant. He didn't want to paint her cousin looking pale and lifeless, but unfortunately that was often how Anne de Bourgh looked in real life.

"The only time I have seen her look quite happy was at the Ashford Races," Georgiana offered. "She likes horses."

"Perhaps I could set up my easel there." He smiled ruefully. "But I doubt your aunt would approve."

Lady Catherine herself entered the room just then, accompanied by Lord and Lady Trisby, two other guests who were staying at Rosings.

Mr. Turner straightened up. "Lady Catherine. How do you do this morning?"

"Not at all well, I am afraid. The pressure is quite distressing. I always know when these summer storms are coming; I am known for it. I invited Mr. and Mrs. Collins to come early for dinner, and we shall all play whist."

"That sounds a delightful plan."

"You must join us."

"Ah. I don't usually—"

"I need a fourth for the second table and must insist that you oblige me."

His face tightened a little, but he responded courteously. "Of course, thank you."

"And you, Georgiana," Lady Catherine continued, "must play as well. You cannot always be retiring to your room when we have guests. I don't know what you learned in your seminary, but you must learn how to go on in company before your debut in London."

Georgiana felt a spurt of anger. Must her aunt say all this in front of her guests? In front of Mr. Turner? "Of course," she said with what dignity she could muster. "I enjoy whist."

"Loo is the all thing now," said Lady Trisby. "One more hand is dealt, which you—"

"*I* have always played whist," interrupted Lady Catherine.

There was a slight silence.

Mr. Turner cleared his throat. "By the by, Miss Darcy, you have not yet shown me your portfolio. I should be happy to offer you any small pointers I can."

"There is no need," Georgiana demurred. "Only sketches…"

"Nonsense, of course it's no trouble to him," Lady Catherine said. "He can't be painting all day, and you are used to having the instruction of art and music masters, are you not? Anne was too ill for such pursuits, unfortunately, but I daresay she would have been excellent if she had had such opportunities. She has a discerning eye for color and design."

"She does," Georgiana agreed.

Georgiana's companion, Mrs. Annesley, cleared her throat. "But I must insist on another time for an art lesson. Miss Darcy must practice the pianoforte if she will be occupied later this afternoon."

Georgiana did not need reminding to practice; she loved playing. She sat at the instrument, the drawing room blessedly empty, and ran her fingers over the ivory keys. She missed her own piano at Pemberley! It was exquisite in tone. Truly, it was too good for her, but her brother had always spoilt her with things of that sort.

This piano was perfectly fine. There was another in the housekeeper's sitting room, but it played distinctly flat. Georgiana began one of her favorite pieces, a sonata by

Dussek she had memorized during her last year at the ladies' seminary she attended in Bath.

She had last played it for Mr. Wickham. When she had gone to Ramsgate for a holiday with her former, and tragically untrustworthy, companion, he had spent many evenings in her company. The sonata had been ruined for her, but today she felt ready to play it again. This was one of her favorite pieces and she would not let it be lost to her.

Wickham or no Wickham.

But... but how she wished Ramsgate had never happened!

Wickham had acted so surprised to see her. So pleased and pleasing. So flatteringly interested in her, her life, and her interests. When Mr. Wickham had finally bullied her into playing for him, oh-so-kindly and winningly, he had given her one of those looks. Those deep looks that seemed to say that he understood her. He did not fulsomely praise her, as she would have hated, but seemed instinctively to know that she loved the music itself, not the display.

She had felt both the comfort of an old acquaintance— someone she associated with the happy days of her childhood and her parents—and the tingly excitement of her first true partiality for a man.

How stupid she had been! How indiscreet!

She had felt thrillingly grown up to have a gentleman call on her in Ramsgate. And Mr. Wickham was so handsome, so heroic-looking! It had perhaps seemed a little strange that her companion should allow him to visit her unaccompanied, but then he was such an old friend. They had both reassured her, and in truth, she had not needed much reassurance. In the country, one did not stand on such forms of propriety as she now learned was common in London.

Georgiana had played this piece for him on the night he had proposed that they elope.

She should have known better. How could Wickham have convinced her to deceive her brother? To throw all caution to the wind? It was blindingly obvious in hindsight, and she felt her soul writhe in shame at what he must have been thinking that whole time.

The gullible Georgiana. The rich, naïve Miss Darcy.

Her hands hit three chords wrong in a row. She stopped with a sigh and began again at the beginning. She loved this song. She must learn to play it without thinking such unpleasant thoughts.

She would think about her brother and Miss Bennet, or Lizzy rather. Georgiana was ecstatic at the thought of their marriage, but there was no one here to discuss it with. Lady Catherine was still furious with Lizzy, and it seemed indelicate to broach the topic with Anne.

But Georgiana's brother was a wonderful man, and that he should have a wife he loved was a true sign of a beneficial Providence, even if there was no one here to rejoice in it with her. Except for her dear Mrs. Annesley, of course, who was still a little stiff about the future Mrs. Darcy. She and Georgiana had suspected for several years that Miss

Caroline Bingley would be the new Mrs. Darcy, however, and Georgiana was sure they were both relieved that it would not be so.

The prospect of having Lizzy to become part of their family… It nearly brought tears to her eyes. And Lizzy would be the one to chaperone Georgiana and introduce her during her season!

Georgiana's first season, including the court presentation and the balls she would attend, was still a matter of dread, but she thought perhaps with Lizzy at her side she would contrive to get through it. Lizzy was bold. She was afraid of nothing. She was beautiful and witty and very kind. Georgiana had whole-heartedly forgiven her for rejecting Darcy the first time he asked her to marry him. Everyone made mistakes—witness Ramsgate!—and Lizzy's mistake was only of the cautious sort.

It was indeed a serious thing for a woman to commit herself to a man, and better to be too careful, like Lizzy, than careless like Georgiana.

Perhaps they would even have children in the next few years. Georgiana liked young children. They were so undemanding and did not stare at her in a way that made her sure whatever topic of conversation she chose would be gauche or boring. They liked to talk of real things, like creeks and fishing and dolls and stories. They did not care if she was witty or clever.

Georgiana made it through the whole sonata this time. She was still playing with absorption an hour later when

A True Likeness

Mrs. Annesley called her to change her dress and join the others in the lower drawing room for cards.

{ 2 }

L ADY CATHERINE TOLD EVERYONE where to sit. It might be the custom in most homes to allow your guests to make up the pairs as they chose, but Lady Catherine did not like to leave decisions lying about for others to pick up.

She put herself opposite Lady Trisby's husband, a very astute player; and her parson, Mr. Collins, was to play opposite Lady Trisby, who was middling.

Anne never played whist; she said it made her head hurt and she could never keep track of the sets.

Lady Catherine had deliberated before including Mr. Turner in her drawing rooms. The social position of an artist, even a member of the Royal Academy, was something of a quandary. They were genteel, of course, and often moved in the highest circles. But there was still the undeniable fact that they were there partly on sufferance, for the skill they possessed and sold for their livelihood. Then there were his absurd religious beliefs. But while she herself would never stoop to basing her behavior on others, she had it on good authority that her life-long friend, Mrs. Winkleigh, considered him perfectly unexceptionable.

The next table, therefore, consisted of Mrs. Collins partnered with Mr. Turner, and Georgiana, partnered with Mr. Sutherland.

This latter was technically a neighbor, though Lady Catherine did not know him well; a large, friendly gentleman about the same age as her nephew Darcy. He seemed rather older than Darcy, however, probably due to marrying at a young age and becoming a widower with a young son before he was thirty. He was friends with Lord Trisby but previously known to Lady Catherine mainly by his property in Surrey, which was large and only touched her own in one small extension. Also, her late husband, Sir Richard, had respected the elder Mr. Sutherland.

The young Mr. Sutherland had visited recently to discuss purchasing the strip of land which adjoined his own estate and had shown pleasing respect for her age and position in the community. During that visit, just after Darcy's engagement—when the average woman would have spurned business matters, probably prostrate with disappointment—Lady Catherine had instead seen opportunity.

Even when under stress, her mind was never still—she was constantly aware of a desire to improve the people and circumstances around her—and it had occurred to her that he would be an excellent husband for Georgiana. He was not titled, but he was the height of respectability: landed, old family, and local. And he would effectively remove Georgiana from the contaminating influence of Elizabeth Bennet.

That was a clear necessity. No niece of hers would be mentored and presented by a treacherous, conniving, impertinent slip of a girl who had bewitched her nephew.

No, Lady Catherine was still smarting over that disaster which had occurred right under her nose. Arranging a beneficial marriage for Georgiana offered a certain salve. She had invited the Trisbys to round out the party. In the meantime, Mr. Sutherland and Georgiana might grow acquainted over the course of the week.

The girl was far too retiring, however. She barely said anything to Mr. Sutherland, and twice she had excused herself from the evening entertainment. Lady Catherine looked with satisfaction on the arrangements for this evening nonetheless. She left nothing to chance.

Mr. Turner was not an adept at whist; he was not a regular card player and despised gambling. However, he was an intelligent man, and Mrs. Collins, his partner, was undemanding. She made matter-of-fact conversation on the weather and the latest news about young Princess Charlotte. She sometimes complimented the others on their play, and occasionally offered mild suggestions as to how he might improve his own.

Georgiana, or Miss Darcy rather, sat very straight as she played. Her cheeks were a little pink, and he wondered if she was still embarrassed about the scold her aunt had given her in the library. He'd heard the muffled tones of her music practice for the past hour and had been tempted to go down and listen. Her "practice" was far superior to what he often heard in posh drawing rooms.

"Your play, Mr. Turner."

"Oh, yes." He discarded a low heart, trying to remember whether his partner had followed suit the last time he played a heart.

Mr. Sutherland shook his head, affably. "No, no, Mrs. Collins trumped your last heart, sir, which means she has no more and you can't count on another quick save. But your loss is our gain." He smiled at Georgiana as she took the trick.

These kinds of evenings, or afternoons rather, were not something he enjoyed. Being a painter, particularly doing portraits of the "upper ten thousand," as the highest ranks of English families were called, meant walking a fine social line. He was not exactly a guest, but neither was he on the level of a tenant or tradesman. Perhaps he was best compared to Mr. Collins, the rector who lived in the nearby parsonage. In the brief time that Mr. Turner had stayed at Rosings, he'd noticed that Mr. Collins and his wife were both summoned and dismissed at the whim of Lady Catherine. He supposed that was not uncommon with great ladies and their parsons.

In the same way, Mr. Turner must always hold himself ready to meet a social gap, but never push further than what was asked. He must be ready to accept invitations with alacrity and snubs with indifference.

When the card games were over, Mr. Sutherland cracked his knuckles and looked at Miss Darcy. "I do miss games of an evening, such a cozy activity on a rainy day."

They followed Lady Catherine to the dining room. She'd suggested (or required) that they sit with their whist partner, and so he found himself again with Mrs. Collins. They were the last to enter the dining room. She looked rather alarmingly unwell as the braised beef was brought in. He glanced at her husband, but he was telling Miss de Bourgh how well she looked after her stay at the Wells.

Mr. Turner leaned slightly toward his partner. "Mrs. Collins, are you feeling quite the thing? Can I get you something?"

She shook her head. Her lips were pushed tightly together and one hand rested low on her midsection.

Mr. Turner, himself the oldest of a large family, immediately guessed the probable cause.

"Perhaps a little wine? Or lemon water?"

Her eyebrows rose at this common remedy for nausea, but she sighed. "You are very observant. I don't want to trouble Lady Catherine, however." Her eyes lingered on her husband, and Mr. Turner wondered if she was, in fact, in the family way, and if so, whether her husband knew of it yet.

She gasped and closed her eyes, pressing a handkerchief to her mouth for a moment.

"If you will not think it too strange, I can offer you the water that happens to be in my glass," he said softly. "And there is a lemon slice just there that you could drop in."

"I would like to say no," she said, "but I do feel very awful and I don't wish to make a scene."

He casually picked up her wine glass instead of his own, scooting his closer to her, and after a brief hesitation, she took his, dropped in the lemon, and sipped it slowly.

No one was paying them any mind. He and Mrs. Collins were definitely the least important people in this gathering, so he ventured to add, "My mother often found lemon water to be a helpful remedy. I am the oldest of eleven, you see, seven living."

"Seven, goodness." She smiled weakly, taking another sip. "Thank you again; that was kind. May I ask why you are drinking water?"

He inclined his head a little. "I am a Methodist."

Her brows rose. "Ah. That explains it."

He waited, but she did not make any other response. There were Methodists in all levels of society these days, but it could not be denied that it was less common in the higher ranks. Also, she was the wife of an acting Anglican rector.

"Is Lady Catherine aware?" she asked eventually. "I only ask because she is a lady of somewhat... decided opinions."

Now it was his turn to smile. "She is aware. She had much to say, but I think she reconciled employing me on the grounds that a Methodist teetotaler is a safely puritanical person to allow close to her daughter."

Mrs. Collins chuckled. "Ah. It is in fact an aid to your career, then?"

Mr. Turner grimaced. On the contrary, many of his denomination, including his mother, questioned whether he could be a portraitist for the elite and also a good Methodist. Herself a devoted follower of the Wesleys, his mother held grave doubts about the circles he was being drawn into. None of this he said to Mrs. Collins, however, merely shaking his head with a rueful smile.

He did not drink any of the wine now in front of him, but he noticed that Georgiana drained her glass twice, which was unusual for her.

The storm which had threatened all day finally broke around eight in the evening and it was still raining heavily when Mr. and Mrs. Collins made their way out to the de Bourgh carriage in the rain. They departed with much thanks to Lady Catherine for her consideration in ordering the carriage—as if she would make them walk home in a downpour!—and the rest of the party sought their beds.

GEORGIANA HERSELF WENT to bed after the card party with a raw throat. It had begun to burn at dinner, and no amount of orgeat seemed to soothe it. She prepared herself in the morning, feeling feverish and uncomfortable, and upon leaving her room was instantly commanded to go back and not to emerge for fear of infecting Anne.

Georgiana was happy to do this, but after lying on her bed for an hour, drowsy but sleepless, she decided to get up.

She went back to the pianoforte in the drawing room. Anne did not play, and thus surely, the risk of infection was minimal.

Being Sunday, Georgiana selected a mass by Haydn from the thick but unorganized book of loose sheet music that she unearthed from the bottom of a forgotten cabinet. She slowly played her way through it, stumbling more than a little. She found one portion which she liked particularly and spent some time getting the melody under her fingers.

A polite cough alerted her to Mr. Turner's presence.

Georgiana looked up in surprise.

"Good morning, Miss Darcy," he said. "Please don't mind me. I merely left a book on the side table there."

He retrieved the book, black and well-bound.

"Is that—is that a hymnal?" Georgiana asked through the dry burn in her throat, reading the words stamped on the front.

"Oh, you sound as if you have a cold," he said. "Why aren't you resting?"

Georgiana shrugged. "I thought everyone was at services."

"I wasn't referring to infection, I only meant that you must feel miserable."

She rubbed the ivory keys. "I can feel miserable anywhere, but at least here I am distracted."

"Ah." He seemed to remember the book in his hands and showed it to her. "Yes, it is a hymnal."

She held it in her hands and flipped it open. His name was written neatly on the leaf, John Wesley Turner. "Oh, you were named after Mr. Wesley, the preacher. I know very little about such things, but I believe there is a Methodist congregation in Lambton, the town near my home. This is why you are not at the Hunsford church?"

"That is correct."

Georgiana had noticed his absence the previous two Sundays, but assumed it was merely disinclination, not conscience. Many young men did not attend services regularly, she knew; Mr. Wickham had happened to be honest about that.

She flipped through the hymns. "Do you play?"

"Yes, some. But I only read the words during my morning devotional."

Georgiana shivered and pulled her shawl a little tighter. "I've heard Methodists are devoted to music. The instrument is free if you would like to play."

"No, thank you. And I must say, I do think you ought to retire. This room is cold; the morning sun doesn't shine in here. You ought to at least go to an east-facing room if you are determined to stay up."

Georgiana smiled wistfully. "At Pemberley the music room faces south and there is always the best light."

"You sound quite homesick."

"Yes, I am. But my brother will be escorting me home in two weeks, at the end of June." Georgiana rose and handed the hymnal back to him.

She felt suddenly light-headed and placed her hand on the piano while the world tipped. Black spots grew at the edges of her vision.

He held her elbow while she steadied herself. "As your brother is not here, I must insist that you rest."

She blinked her eyes until the room was still again. "Clearly, I ought."

He escorted her back to her room, and she was too tired to consider if that was proper.

"Can I summon Mrs. Annesley for you?"

"No, I insisted she go on to the church. She is very devout and hates to miss it. She will be back presently, with the others, and will look in on me then."

John went slowly back to the library, which had been his original destination when he heard Miss Darcy playing and made retrieving the book an excuse to speak with her.

He found Mr. Sutherland settled in the library already, seated by the fire with a periodical. John bade him a good morning and continued out onto the terrace.

He pitied Georgiana; falling ill was always worse when away from home, but she would no doubt be fine in a few days. He wondered again why she was staying here just now. It seemed that Lady Catherine had had some sort of falling out with Georgiana's older brother and would hardly speak his name. Anne and Georgiana did not appear to be particular friends, either, which increased the awkwardness of her position.

And unless he was much mistaken, Lady Catherine was hoping to arrange a match between Georgiana and Mr. Sutherland, the young widower.

It had nothing to do with him, of course. These glimpses into people's lives were just that, glimpses. In a few weeks he would go back to London, and from thence to the next portrait project that had been commissioned. Several of his pieces had been displayed at the Royal Academy presentation at Somerset House last year, and he had gained a certain amount of notoriety since then.

Miss Darcy had asked about his plans only a few days ago, and he had explained how recommendations were the bread-and-butter of an artist such as himself, leading from commission to commission with hopefully few long gaps between. Miss Darcy herself—

But John stopped himself, he must not be continually thinking of that young lady. He could only assume his slight preoccupation formed because she was the only person in this house who was interested in art. Lady Catherine wanted the portrait, of course, but that was a matter of status. Miss Darcy actually enjoyed the process of it—how to prepare the canvases, which were the best powders and clay for the colors, the type of oil to be used, and the steps from sketch to underpainting to glaze. Much of oil painting was technical; many people did not realize that.

John resolutely turned his thought to pious matters and spent the remainder of the morning in solitude.

He was still on the terrace when Mr. Sutherland stuck his head out the door. "Care for a luncheon? The family is back and assembling in the dining room."

"Yes, I will come."

"How is the portrait coming along?" Mr. Sutherland asked.

"Well, thank you. A few more sittings and it will be complete."

"Fast, aren't you? My wife wanted a family portrait and I swear the man spent months on it merely to batten himself at our expense."

John made a non-committal noise.

"Of course, I didn't begrudge it to her. Now that she's gone, I'm thankful to have that painting. Influenza," he added. His round face looked as if it ought to smile, not bear the look of real grief John saw there now.

"I'm sorry."

He inclined his head. "Hard to believe it's been four years, but I have a little boy; time I moved on."

John nodded. His surmises about the man and Georgiana were probably correct, then. And it could be worse; he seemed a good-natured man. Perhaps she would be happy with him. A chance statement had made him think that she did not want a grand match and rather dreaded the London season that was planned for her. Perhaps she would prefer to settle early, as some did, and avoid it altogether.

And *again*, it had nothing to do with him.

Georgiana convalesced and was glad to leave her room and rejoin the world of Rosings by Wednesday evening. The Collinses had been invited again, and Georgiana found herself next to Mrs. Collins after dinner, while the gentlemen finished their port.

Though of course, she remembered, Mr. Turner would not drink anything alcoholic if he was a Methodist. Did he only drink tea and water? How strange.

Mrs. Collins touched her hand while Lady Catherine and Lady Trisby were occupied at the other end of the room. "Miss Darcy, I have not yet had the chance to tell you how happy I am about your brother's engagement. Lizzy has been my best friend since I can remember and I think they will deal extremely well together."

Georgiana felt warmth bubbling up in her. "Yes, I do as well. I do not know her like you, but I enjoyed her company prodigiously in Tunbridge."

"Lizzy is always laughing," Mrs. Collins said. "She is better than a tonic for low-spirits."

"I don't know that I heard her laugh so often in Tunbridge, but I can well believe it is so."

"I suppose she was preoccupied. She certainly had no idea when she left here that Mr. Darcy would… that he was at all approving of her. In fact, she thought he disliked her since the outset of their acquaintance. That was the root of the trouble, I believe."

Georgiana enjoyed a quiet gossip with Mrs. Collins, learning more than she expected about Lizzy and her brother's first meeting and subsequent friendship.

When the gentlemen joined them, Mr. Turner wandered to the pianoforte and leafed through the music, catching the end of their conversation. "Did I meet Mr. Darcy in Tunbridge?" he asked. "I cannot recall."

When Georgiana looked up, she was surprised to see that Anne had also moved quite near. Georgiana hoped that

Anne had not overheard all of their conversation. She did not seem to like Lizzy very much.

Mr. Turner repeated his question.

"Oh, no, I do not think you met my brother," Georgiana answered, trying to remember. "He generally did not accompany us to the bath house where you were painting. You met Miss Bennet, though perhaps you do not remember. She was always with Anne and I."

"I do remember."

Lady Catherine had approached without their noticing. "What do you remember? What are you speaking of over here?"

Mr. Turner looked unsure of what to say and Mrs. Collins, who knew of Lady Catherine's anger over the match, remained silent. Georgiana hated conflict, but she also despised falsehood. "We were speaking of my brother's engagement."

Lady Catherine's face became hawk-like and she made a sound between a snort and a cough. "Foolishness. That is what it is. I should not like to say so of my own nephew, but I must say that he has been foolish not to heed the warnings of his elders."

Georgiana thought perhaps they might escape with only that animadversion, but Lady Catherine sat in her throne-like chair in the grouping around the pianoforte and continued. "As for Miss Elizabeth Bennet! Well. I was never more mistaken in a person. It does not happen often, so I can only conclude that there is some deep duplicity in her character. I cannot wholly exonerate my nephew, however. He has turned his back on the duties of rank and family. He allied himself with a mere *Miss Bennet*, a companion to Anne no less, with no rank, pedigree, or even gentility to recommend her."

Mrs. Collins did not look happy, and Georgiana, usually the gentlest of girls, was growing angry. "My brother has not turned his back on anything. If he loves Miss Elizabeth, then— then he ought to marry her."

Lady Catherine raised her brows.

John did not like the direction this was going and rather thought Miss Darcy was about to be excoriated by her aunt for venturing to disagree with her.

Miss Darcy had only today left her bedroom, and her voice still sounded worn. The Trisbys and Mr. Sutherland were also joining the group, and John felt a sort of protective instinct to turn the conversation away from Miss Darcy.

"Do you play the pinaoforte, Miss de Bourgh?" he asked, pretending to be oblivious to the fact that Lady Catherine was about to reply.

"Anne's health has always been delicate; she could not dedicate herself to the usual accomplishments," Lady Catherine snapped.

Mr. Sutherland spoke up, "I do enjoy music of an evening. Miss Darcy, you play, do you not?" He sat himself next to Miss de Bourgh.

"Yes, do play for us," Lady Catherine agreed, grudgingly giving up her diatribe. "Since Mr. Sutherland enjoys music."

Miss Darcy sat herself at the piano without the usual polite excuses young ladies gave before playing. She must be happy to end the conversation as well.

Georgiana immediately began to play a piece for which, apparently, she did not need music, and Lady Catherine began a monologue which apparently did not need silence.

Her topics ranged from Miss Darcy's many fine accomplishments to Miss Darcy's substantial inheritance to her select education. Clearly the information was for Mr. Sutherland's benefit, for there would be no reason to offer this lecture to himself or the Trisbys. Georgiana could hear it all, and her face grew pale. Her fingers, though still finding the notes, had occasional hesitations and stumbles.

When she finished the song, she rose to the polite applause of the guests. "Thank you, but please excuse me. I think I shall retire before tea; I still find myself rather tired."

Mrs. Annesley came at once to escort her to her room, and John was left with the rest of the party for the duration of the evening. He realized with dismay that he was disappointed Miss Darcy was gone. He'd unconsciously been looking forward to her return to health to relieve the tedium of these evenings. And why was it less tedious with her? She was not a great talker, though they always exchanged a few words over tea and sometimes ended in discussion of the relative merit of realism vs. romanticism or English composers vs. German, or something of that sort.

The truth was that just her presence made everything more agreeable. And that was very stupid. In his career, John could not fancy himself in love with every pretty girl who enjoyed the same things he did. Not that he was in love with Miss Darcy, but it would be fatally easy to…

No, he must immediately stop thinking of her like this.

{ 4 }

GEORGIANA'S HEALTH IMPROVED over the next few days and she was glad to join Anne, Mr. Turner, and Mrs. Annesley in the library during Anne's next sitting.

It was necessary for Mrs. Annesley to be there, because Anne's own companion, Mrs. Jenkinson, was still away with family. Lizzy had been Anne's companion briefly, but that had ended abruptly when Lizzy and Fitzwilliam became engaged. Georgiana wasn't sure what vexed Lady Catherine more: that Lizzy had become engaged to Darcy while employed by herself, or that Darcy had taken Lady Catherine severely to task for being rude to Lizzy and her family.

Georgiana sat a little a part and watched Mr. Turner paint. He had sketched in Anne's face, dress, and limbs onto the canvas from his previous sketches. Today, with the good light, he was getting the shadows and highlights refined with an underpainting of various shades of umber.

Mr. Sutherland and Lady Catherine also came up to join them and they chatted with Mrs. Annesley about the summer planting and the weather they were likely to have.

Georgiana had finally understood, while she played the piano Wednesday night, what her aunt was thinking in regard to Mr. Sutherland. Perhaps Georgiana ought to have realized sooner, but her brother knew how hurt and confused she'd been after Ramsgate and had told her that he would not rush her into marriage. In fact, he'd pointed out that as a considerable heiress herself, she need not marry if she did not choose to.

But of course, Lady Catherine knew nothing about the fiasco at Ramsgate, and she felt that Georgiana ought to marry, and marry well. Would it always be this way? Why did so many persons care whom Georgiana might marry? Only a few weeks ago, she had been thrown into anxiety by Caroline Bingley's insinuations that Georgiana should marry *her* brother, Charles! That, at least, had turned out to be nothing. Charles was safely engaged to Lizzy's sister Jane, which was another source of joy to Georgiana, who had taken an instant liking to Lizzy's beautiful older sister.

And before Mr. Bingley, of course, there had been Wickham, who had nearly secured her hand and fortune for himself.

Was this what her life would be like if she never married? People always trying to sway her to their choice?

It was almost enough to make her choose marriage only to avoid all these machinations! It was because she was wealthy, she knew. She did not want to be destitute, of course, but she rather thought that to be, say, a young lady of moderate prospects like the Bennet sisters would be quite pleasant.

It was not to be, however. She must either marry or avoid marriage all her life.

But to marry… she could not picture trusting anyone enough to do so. Not after feeling like such a fool with Wickham. Her first love, her first *kiss*—how indiscreet she had been!—all based on a deception.

If she was ever to marry, it would have to be with someone incurably honest. And maybe not so handsome and fashionable as Wickham. Definitely someone who did not want to cut a figure in London, because Georgiana did not think she would ever enjoy that sort of thing. Love would be nice, too, but then she had thought she loved Wickham, so perhaps that was as foolish as Lady Catherine said it was.

"Miss Darcy, could you pull back that curtain for us?" Mr. Turner asked, gesturing with his paintbrush at one of the drapes over the terrace windows.

She went immediately to the window and drew it back, but the tie was lost or gone, and it was too thick to twist to the side and stay back.

"Hm. Could you perhaps just hold it there for a moment?" he asked. "I won't be long."

She obediently held it back, though it was less interesting from this angle because she could not see the painting.

She could see Mr. Turner, however, and his eyes flicking ever so quickly back and forth between his subject and his painting.

"There," he said after a few moments. "That will do nicely for today." He hunted around for a rag to wipe his hands. "Thank you, Miss de Bourgh, Miss Darcy."

Georgiana came around to see the painting while he absently rubbed a few dark smudges of paint off his hands and wrists. His hands were square and stocky, rather like the rest of him, but when they held a paintbrush, it seemed like he could paint the individual hairs on a caterpillar.

"Are you satisfied with his progress?" Mr. Sutherland asked her.

Georgiana did not turn, though she felt a bit rude. "I wouldn't know," she said.

"But your aunt says you enjoy all sorts of art yourself. All young ladies do, do they not?"

"I suppose," Georgiana said vaguely. She did not want to encourage Mr. Sutherland. Why did they not teach this in her deportment classes, instead of the angle at which to pour tea for a duchess?

Lady Catherine intervened. "Georgiana, you look pale. You ought to walk or ride more often or you will not regain your strength."

"Yes, ma'am. I daresay you're right."

"A ride would be the thing for today," Mr. Sutherland agreed. "Miss de Bourgh, Miss Darcy, I offer myself as an escort."

Mr. Turner knelt down and began to clean his brushes with a strong-smelling turpentine. Thick cloths protected the handsome carpet.

Georgiana felt a bit trapped. Neither she or her brother could have guessed that Lady Catherine would seek to make a match for her like this. Not that Georgiana had anything against Mr. Sutherland. He might meet all of her requirements, but even if he was a paragon, she was not ready for this.

"Of course, a wonderful plan for the afternoon," Lady Catherine decided. "Go put on your habit at once, both of you."

Mr. Sutherland looked pleased. "Turner, you care to accompany? You probably need some air as well after all those fumes. Lady Catherine would mount you, I'm sure."

Mr. Turner looked up in surprise at the invitation. "I am fine, sir. No need."

"Yes, go," Lady Catherine said. "We have plenty of horses and they do not get enough exercise."

Georgiana brightened at that. She was not sure what showed on her face, but when she went to her room to put on her riding habit, Mrs. Annesley followed.

"My dear," she said slowly. "I feel I need to caution you."

"About Mr. Sutherland?"

Her companion blinked. "No. About Mr. Turner."

"Oh."

Mrs. Annesley busied herself getting out Georgiana's gloves, handkerchief, and whip. "It is natural that you feel some interest in his profession, and some preference for him as a previous acquaintance from your school days."

"I can hardly say we were acquainted then," Georgiana said. "He was only doing a favor for his aunt, my arts mistress."

"For whatever reason, you seem to prefer his company to most others. He seems to be a polite, well-spoken young man, but you must be careful."

"I haven't been... been inappropriate somehow, have I?" Georgiana felt a little ill at the thought.

"No, not at all." Mrs. Annesley laid a compassionate hand on her shoulder. "You always behave as you ought. I am only anxious lest your emotions mislead you to your own hurt, not that they will mislead you into wrong action."

"I am not aware... that is, I like Mr. Turner, certainly. He is easy to talk to and very interesting, of course, but I have no further thoughts of... anything."

"How many people do you find easy to talk to?" Mrs. Annesley's voice became muffled as she turned away to retrieve a hat from inside the bureau, the hat that matched Georgiana's riding dress.

"Not... many."

"Exactly." She put the hatbox on the bed. "For quiet young ladies, it is sometimes a short step between ease of conversation and girlish fancy."

Georgiana smoothed her skirt, a bit hurt. "I am aware. I have told you about M-Mr. Wickham," she stumbled. "You know that I realize how at fault I was."

"Oh, my dear Miss Darcy." She took Georgiana's hands in her own. "I am not trying to scold you. That man was a wicked cad, and *he* deceived *you*. I am concerned now because Mr. Turner is a very good sort of man, only he is… not the sort of man for you. He is talented and gentlemanly, but that is not quite the same as being a gentleman. He is not a guest here, you know. There is a difference."

"I had no such thoughts about Mr. Turner," Georgiana said, quite honestly. Though now she felt inexplicably sad. It was unfortunate that she could not be an ordinary Miss Smith or Miss Johnson, of nowhere in particular, who might be interested in a plain Mr. Turner.

"Good. I shouldn't want you to give any more of your heart away. He is not exactly a tradesman, of course, but Mr. Darcy would never find him acceptable."

"He is a Methodist, besides," Georgiana added.

"Even more reason." Mrs. Annesley felt all dissenters were a step from apostasy.

Georgiana finished getting ready. "Do you have any warnings for me about Mr. Sutherland? Is it my imagination that my aunt is encouraging me to spend time with him?"

She frowned. "No, it is not your imagination. Mr. Darcy will not appreciate her attempting to arrange such a thing for you, though I am sure I have nothing against the gentleman. If you liked him, he might be the very... Have you put this matter in your letters?"

"No. I did not realize at first... and I'm certain my brother is busy with Miss Elizabeth's family at present. I would not want to bother him; he might feel he ought to come get me."

Georgiana had offered to stay with Lady Catherine, and she knew her brother had only reluctantly accepted. Lady Catherine had been so unpleasant at the time of his engagement! Her anger was hot, and it had found outlet in the (somewhat) legitimate complaint that Lizzy was leaving Anne without the vestige of a chaperone, after making an agreement to remain until Mrs. Jenkinson returned.

Georgiana, sensing finally a way in which she might repay her brother for his kindness, had offered herself. If she were to stay with Lady Catherine, along with Mrs. Annesley, who accompanied Georgiana everywhere, Anne would be amply chaperoned. Darcy had been startled, but it truly had been the best solution, and he had eventually thanked her for being so thoughtful of her cousin.

Of course, it was not for Anne at all, it was for Darcy, but if it made his summer with Elizabeth better, that was enough for her. She'd rather thought he might press the issue, but it seemed he was not overly eager for her to spend extended time with Lizzy's family. Nor was Georgiana eager to spend the intervening weeks with Caroline Bingley!

"You are never a bother to him," Mrs. Annesley said, "but I think you will be fine to wait. Only two more weeks, and Mr. Sutherland does not seem excessively particular. I believe it is more your aunt's desire than his intention."

{ 5 }

AFTER THE GROOM HELPED Georgiana and Anne to mount, they set out south, following the road which led to the village. It was a warm, still day. The fields were green, not yet ripe, and the ditch grasses ended in buds that had not yet tasseled. There were puffy white clouds that were surprisingly thick when they drifted in front of the sun, and the sun was all the brighter when it came out again.

Mr. Sutherland complimented them both on their style and added that Miss de Bourgh was looking quite restored since her stay in Tunbridge Wells. He naturally asked about the environs of Rosings as they passed by various fields and tenant cottages and thankfully, Anne knew far more about the region than Georgiana did.

They could not ride four abreast down the lane, so Georgiana fell back next to Mr. Turner. They were in turn followed by the groom who was accompanying them in case

Anne should grow overly tired or some other accident occurred.

Georgiana wished traitorously that Mrs. Annesley had said nothing. Mr. Turner always felt safe, in some indefinable fashion, but now she had to be on her guard. How distasteful!

He seemed to be in a quiet, contemplative mood, however, so she was able to enjoy the ride with relatively little guilt.

Mr. Sutherland's questions about Rosings gradually turned to questions about Pemberley and Lambton. Georgiana wondered whether he was politely including her in the conversation or desiring to learn more of her background and wealth. How tiresome it was to be an adult!

She traded places with Anne for a bit, resigned to holding up her end of the conversation. Thankfully it occurred to her to ask about Mr. Sutherland's own estate.

In talking about that, he had much to say. He was introducing new improvements and efficiencies, and when Georgiana invited him to explain, he went so far as to describe the small experimental farm he had designed and built for his own ideas. "It is probably not very interesting to you, however," he said, recalling himself before he'd gone on too long. "My property adjoins your aunt's in one small corner, but the bulk of it lies in Surrey, and the house itself is less than a few hours from London."

"I suppose that is convenient."

A True Likeness

"Yes, my wife enjoyed spending most of the season in London, and since I could post down once a week to check on things at home, it worked splendidly."

"I do not care for London," Georgiana said coldly, but then she felt bad for responding that way to his reminiscence of his late wife. "I am sorry for your loss."

"Thank you. I regret her for my own sake, but even more for Barney's."

"Barney?"

"My son. Did Lady Catherine not mention him?"

"No. How—how old is he?"

"Nearing five. His nanny has him well in hand, but I am very fond of my own mother and I regret that he has lost that."

"My mother died when I was five," Georgiana said. She hurried on, "But I am sure Barney's grandparents must dote on him."

"Yes, my own mother lives with us and last year he spent many winter months with his maternal grandparents."

"I'm sure he couldn't want for more." Georgiana didn't want her sympathy to be excited towards Mr. Sutherland. It was hard enough to try and hint any man away—so awkward!—but it was a thousand times worse if she didn't want to hurt his feelings.

After they went through the village, Anne suggested they go back through the fields and circle back from the east. No one objected, and as Anne knew the way, Georgiana was allowed to fall back again.

The clouds made delightful patches of dark on the quilted fields. Farther away, one of her aunt's orchards stretched in pleasing lines, the trees vibrantly but unevenly green with dark old foliage and bright new growth.

"Pretty as a picture, isn't it?" Mr. Turner remarked. "I can see why Kent is called the Garden of England."

"Yes. Do you live in London?" Georgiana asked abruptly.

"Ah—yes. I have rooms on Upper Bradbury Street."

Georgiana blushed at her forwardness. "London looms rather inescapable in my mind just now." She gestured to the fields, tucking her knee more securely in the sidesaddle. "Do you ever paint landscapes?"

"As a student I did. I have not recently, as I've made portraiture my focus." He sounded a little regretful.

"Would you go back to it, if you could paint anything?"

"No one has asked me that in a long time. I believe," he laughed, "it is most unlikely, but I should like very much to travel and paint foreign landscapes. I would love to visit America and paint the Catskills and the Adirondacks, perhaps the Hudson River Valley. I met an American painter while I was a student at the Academy and his descriptions nearly had me buying a passage before I reached my majority." He smiled on the fields around them. "This is beautiful, but it has been cultivated for nearly a thousand years. I would love to paint real wilderness."

Georgiana tilted her head. "I cannot picture it, except for the reproductions I have seen in books and newspapers. I can't imagine actually going to such places."

"I can."

His thoughts seemed to be otherwhere, so she allowed the silence to lengthen.

Only when they were nearly back to the house did he look over to her. "I apologize. I was lost in thought."

"No apology is necessary," Georgiana said. Her own thoughts were not precisely clear either.

John rather thought he'd brushed through the ride tolerably well. He had not meant to get carried away talking about his dreams, but other than that, it had been fine.

He had reckoned without Lady Catherine's desire to make full use of those around her.

"Georgiana, have you shown your sketchbook to Mr. Turner yet?" she demanded later that day.

Georgiana responded quietly.

"How silly!" Lady Catherine responded. "He has just been explaining how he must wait for the current layers to dry completely, so why should he not make himself useful to you? Go, at once. I always say there is no time like the present; I am known for it."

Georgiana returned presently with a large portfolio similar to what most girls her age used. It was dark blue with ribbons tying the thick covers shut and a quantity of loose-leaf paper neatly stacked inside.

John had never wanted to be an art instructor. Many poor artists needed to take whatever job they could get, even with a paltry income, so some counted themselves lucky to become a teacher at a girls' school. (Most boys were not encouraged to pursue art, but rather to polish their Latin and literature.) John could conceive of few fates worse than to be stuck teaching listless—and generally talentless—young ladies for years at a time.

He expected better of Miss Darcy, though he could not for the life of him recall any of her work from his brief stay with his aunt. His aunt was the one who had recognized his early skill and persuaded his parents to fund him at the Royal Academy. She wrote him regularly, and he always replied, knowing that she enjoyed living vicariously through his success. As a woman, it was prohibitively difficult to enter the academy or pursue any professional living with her skills, although she was quite talented. When he had gone to visit her, he had been more interested in seeing some of her own work than in that of the contest he was supposed to be judging.

He remembered being relieved that one entry had stood far above the others; and he had a brief recollection of congratulating the winning student. The winning student who had happened to be Miss Darcy.

She untied the book and handed it to him.

{ 6 }

JOHN DID NOT PARTICULARLY WANT to critique Miss Darcy's efforts, but he decidedly did not want to do it within earshot of Lady Catherine. As with many older, autocratic ladies, she seemed oblivious of the finer emotions in others.

"I cannot spread out the papers here without making a nuisance of myself," John said. "Lady Catherine…?"

"Yes, the large table in the morning room. You will bother no one there."

If John were a regular guest, he reflected, she would not send Georgiana off alone with him, but would expect her to have a chaperone. But he was in the guise of art master now, and as such, was apparently no longer considered a man.

If Lady Catherine knew how difficult he found it not to think about Miss Darcy in a warmer light, now that the idea had occurred to him, she would think differently.

Sighing a little, John spread out the portfolio in the empty morning room and began to look through the drawings. Miss Darcy seemed to prefer pencil; most of her work was in black and white, though he spotted a few watercolors at the back.

"These are quite good," he said absently, "as I'm sure you know."

She drew the things that most young ladies did: flowers, fountains, domestic scenes. He flipped through several sheets of flower studies: roses, chrysanthemum, lilies and the like, and came across a page of insects. A butterfly did not surprise him, but a rather hairy spider was followed by a page of fluttering moths and then a rather fat beetle.

He smiled despite himself. "Where did you find these?"

She was standing several feet away, hands clasped together, as if she might be required to recite a lesson.

"We may as well sit," he said, pulling out a chair for her at the table.

"The spider was under the eaves outside my window," she said. "It spun a web just outside the glass, and I had never seen one so large."

"Most girls would demand the gardener kill it."

"If it had been inside, I definitely would have," she admitted.

"And the others?"

"I don't recall each instance, but after the spider, I began to notice them more. My seminary encouraged much time spent out of doors, but Bath is rainy and rather unpleasant.

I did not want to draw dripping signs and wet cobblestones, so I drew these."

He smiled. "Excellent eye for detail. If you were a man, I daresay you could find work as a naturalist, categorizing and illustrating the texts. There is fine work being done on South American insects just now. I saw a display at the Natural History Museum, and it was extraordinary."

She seemed to relax a fraction. "Perhaps I can ask my brother to take me there when we return to London for the season next year. Then I shall have something to look forward to."

He continued looking through the portfolio. She had gone through a phase of portraits. Or perhaps she had been required to by his aunt. There were many sketches and watercolors of girls he assumed were her friends at school.

Then he turned over a leaf that was slightly stuck and found a man's face. He was smiling and leaning forward familiarly, and it was labeled only with a *W.*

She jerked as though shocked. "Oh. I thought I had thrown that out."

It was only polite to keep moving and not ask questions, but he was burning with them. He only allowed himself to ask casually, "Your brother?"

"N-no."

He came across another sketch, this one of a man leaning over a desk, checking a ledger.

"That one is my brother," she said. "The next one is his fiancée, Elizabeth Bennet."

He looked and admired, and even offered a pointer on the relative proportion of foreheads and chins, and the triangle made between the nose and tips of the eyebrows, but his mind was back with that other picture.

It was clear from her reaction that it was someone she formerly cared about. It was clear from the picture that the man was no boy her age; he had the look of a man about town. The drawing was more finished than the others as well. Much time and attention had gone into it. What was such a man doing smiling like that and posing for Miss Darcy?

She was not relaxed any longer, if she ever had been.

"Are you quite well, Miss Darcy?"

"Of course."

"It is only that I have asked many people to sit still in the course of painting them, and none of them have turned quite so statue-like as you have just done." He knew he ought not tease her, but it didn't feel right to let her stew in… whatever emotion was currently upsetting her.

Georgiana thought she had burnt all her sketches of Wickham. She had gone through and done it alone one bleak October day, too ashamed for anyone to know how many she had made.

Mr. Turner did not know the whole story from one picture, but somehow that was worse. The picture was a window into her indiscretion and foolishness.

"He—He was—" Georgiana stopped. Unthinkable to explain that she had nearly eloped at the age of fifteen. "I meant to throw it away," she repeated lamely, unable to explain. To her dismay, she felt tears fill her eyes.

She stood abruptly and walked to the small lady's desk that sat in the corner. She wiped her eyes and looked up and to the left, forcing back her tears. How she wished she could go back in time and take back that entire trip to Ramsgate.

She jumped when she realized that Mr. Turner had come up behind her. He held out a handkerchief, and she took it, blotting her eyes.

"I'm sorry, Miss Darcy. I shouldn't have pushed you."

She shook her head. "It is not your fault. I cannot explain except to say that I did something very foolish and wrong. I keep thinking I have put it behind me, but then something like that comes along to remind me."

"Well, as someone who has done numerous things foolish and wrong," Mr. Turner said slowly, "I know that God is always ready to forgive and to give wisdom."

"I have asked God to forgive me, but I still feel guilty and… and stupid. My brother says it is not my fault, but I do not feel that way." She sniffed and blotted her eyes again.

John wanted to plant his considerable right hook into that man's face. Instead, he said, "If you asked, then God forgave. Any lingering guilt or shame is therefore a deception, not a judgment."

She wiped her nose delicately. "That is a nice thought."

"It is true. But Miss Darcy, I am certain that the fault was not with you at all. And if you were foolish, well, foolishness is not a sin." Whatever had happened was probably not as severe as she thought, not if her brother was still bringing her out next year. A flirtation gone too far, most likely… though the timeline still confused him. She had been in school until recently and was not out. When would any of this have happened?

He shook his head and went back to her portfolio. "May I?" he asked.

"Please."

He found the offending picture and crumpled it up. Using the toe of his boot, he nudged it into the crack between the wood already laid for the next fire. "There, all gone."

She chuckled a little and put his handkerchief back on the table. She began to repack her portfolio. "If only memories could be disposed of so easily."

Again, John felt the urge to hurt someone. How dare that unknown fellow leave Miss Darcy with such memories? At her age?

Without thinking, John found his hand on her shoulder. "Miss Darcy—"

She shook her head sharply, whether to prevent him from speaking or something else, he wasn't sure, but her hand came up and gripped his for a moment.

A True Likeness

Looking into her eyes, John knew he was lost. He wanted to protect her, to take care of her, to make her smile.

He wanted to be the one who made her forget that man. And he very much could not be.

7

*D*EAR GEORGIANA,

    Charlotte tells me you defended Fitzwilliam and I quite nobly; that you contradicted your aunt in front of her guests! It ought to be hymned and sung by a Greek chorus. And you think you are not brave?

Truly, I am impressed, but please do not feel you have to defend me. I don't feel I have yet earned such loyalty! You have my full permission to strategically retreat as necessary, and you are fully prohibited from engaging in any heroic last stands!

I am enmeshed in the details of trousseau and wedding breakfast, as it seems my mother has invited the entire town of Meryton to attend. I can only be thankful that Jane is involved. I freely make use of her planning and practicality. If you should ever choose to marry, we must have her visit and advise us how to go on, because I don't think I shall remember anything useful from this summer.

I love my family—the imminent prospect of leaving them has shown me how much!—but I can also see their faults. I fear this is a rather trying time for your brother. I know he writes you as diligently as always, but do not be dismayed if his letters betray distraction. He is devoting a rather extraordinary amount of will towards not throttling my mother. He does not speak of it to me—perhaps it would be easier if he did!—but I can tell he is struggling. I shan't put you to the blush, but I will agree with what you told me in Tunbridge, that your brother is very good and very patient.

As for the rest, if you should ever choose to marry, I promise not to mention your intended's income more than once a day, and I solemnly promise never to cast myself onto his chest in a paroxysm of thankfulness. You may thank me now, or when the time comes, at your convenience!

Much love,
Lizzy

Georgiana stayed in her room as much as possible for the next few days. What else was one to do when her mind was fixated on someone completely unsuitable?

And Mrs. Annesley had warned her! Georgiana felt the familiar burn of foolishness, but this time it was offset by a sort of misery and excitement.

The misery came when she thought of leaving Rosings in a matter of days, at the end of June, and probably never seeing Mr. Turner again.

The excitement was an uncontrollable thing that made her wake up with exhilaration before remembering that the thing buoying her up was just an air castle. It made her long to see him and talk to him, which she denied herself as best she might. It also made her think of him almost constantly, which she could not deny herself, even when she tried.

The result was that she spent more time with Mr. Sutherland than she had previously. Between the two men, he now seemed by far the less threat to her peace of mind. What could he do, after all?

Mr. Turner was the same as always, as of course he ought to be. He had comforted a silly, crying girl and disposed of a silly, foolish sketch. He probably thought no more of it.

Whereas Georgiana could not eat dinner without noticing the bright blue of his eyes, the frankness in his square face, or the humor in his occasional remarks.

It was hopeless, however; she knew that very well. He was not of the same rank. Her brother had been unsure about marrying Lizzy, and Lizzy was clearly the daughter of a gentleman. Who was Mr. Turner? She actually knew very little; he had mentioned in one of their early conversations that he came from a large family in Sussex.

Even if he was of their station… he dreamed of travel and adventure and excitement. It sounded very uncomfortable and scary to Georgiana, who would be happy to stay at Pemberley for the rest of her life. She only once allowed herself to fantasize the possibility of marrying Mr. Turner.

She was rich, was she not? She could fund his art like a… a patron. On her inheritance, he could even afford to go to the Americas and paint the wilderness or the savages or whatever he desired!

But even in that dream, she could not picture herself there. And when she imagined them here in England, it did not work much better. She could not picture herself in a plain Methodist congregation—were they not rather like Quakers?—or picture how they would live in London.

She was not opposed to his religion necessarily. She had heard her brother sharply criticize the way the Church of England allowed any wastrel to become a priest, in the context of Wickham's expectation of receiving one of the livings that was at Darcy's disposal. "The folly of it is that many would allow him to be ordained," he had said. "And I might install any scoundrel I like. I will not do so, of course, but the system that would allow it is severely flawed."

Georgiana was as pious as most young ladies, she believed, rather more than some. She liked how Mr. Turner spoke of holy things as if they could be known and understood.

But still, the vision of herself and Mr. Turner refused to resolve itself into anything coherent. The barriers were real, and they were implacable.

Furthermore, she did not know whether he thought of her at all. Most likely not, and she would never humiliate herself by alluding to feelings that were unreciprocated and irrelevant.

By repeating these things to herself, Georgiana managed to get through several more rides, two supper parties, and one exceptionally long week.

When her brother rode up to Rosings in his chaise, Georgiana was on the watch. She ran down to the first floor where the butler was waiting to receive him. She did not wait for Darcy to make it to the front door but flew down the shallow steps and hugged him.

"Georgiana! You missed me, I believe?"

"Very much so." She clung to him for a moment, before schooling herself to decorum and accompanying him up the steps. "My aunt will be glad you have come, though she might... she might have more to say about Miss Bennet."

He sighed. "Poor Georgiana. You are a saint for bearing the brunt of her bad humor."

"It has been trying at times, but she has guests, and that has been a welcome distraction."

"Guests?" He shrugged out of his driving cloak and handed it to the butler. "Thank you, Parker."

The butler draped it over his arm. "I believe Lady Catherine is to be found in the upper drawing room, Mr. Darcy. Your things shall be put in your usual room."

"Very good."

With time to look at him, Georgiana saw that her brother was looking rather stressed. Shouldn't he be happier? He got to spend the last month with Lizzy and her family!

Of course, returning to confront Lady Catherine at Rosings would be enough to stress almost anyone, but her brother was not just anyone. He was not intimidated by Lady Catherine's harsh words and looks; therefore, there must be something else.

His look of stress did not dissipate when the introductions were made, and, after a suitable interval, Mr. Sutherland asked to have a word with him.

8

D ARCY WAS RARELY AT A LOSS for words, but this sudden request for Georgiana's hand, by a man a least a year or two older than himself, took him completely by surprise.

"My sister, Georgiana?" Darcy repeated.

"I would normally wait until I could further my acquaintance with you both, but I understand from her that you intend to depart in the morning. And I believe in discussing things right out. I may as well ask you if I can court her now rather than in six months or a year. And I do mean court. I assume you still want her to have her first season, to be presented, and so on."

"I do."

"That is partly why I have spoken now. I assume you will want to make your own inquiries as to my suitability and so on, though I venture to say that Lady Catherine will vouch for me. Sir Richard and my father got along well, you see. Neighbors for generations and whatnot. Lady Catherine has been most encouraging of my suit."

Darcy began to feel quite thunderous. "Has she?"

"Yes." Mr. Sutherland was a rather large man who looked as if he would be more comfortable in homespuns or riding clothes than the current drawing room dress. "I hadn't previously met Miss Darcy—well, how should I, when she is just out?—but Lady Catherine was kind enough to say that she thought we might suit. I know that she is not Miss Darcy's guardian, I only mention that to explain why I have had hope."

"My sister is very young—"

"Yes, that has given me pause. I am not so old myself—"

"How old, if I may ask?" Darcy interrupted.

"I am twenty-eight. And as I say, Miss Darcy's age has given me pause. I'm a widower, and that might very well *not* be what you would wish for her, and I don't blame you. I will only say two things: that she seems to have no desire for a grand match—and I don't say that to better my offer, she said so herself only yesterday—and that she has grown quite friendly over the last few days. That has emboldened me to seek this audience with you."

Very friendly? Georgiana? Darcy felt further and further adrift. "Mr. Sutherland, I appreciate your candor, but I cannot give you any encouragement at this time. Even if Georgiana does not desire a grand match—"

"Or even to be presented," Mr. Sutherland added.

Darcy compressed his lips. "Even so, a true season, un-attached and uncommitted if possible, is what our mother would have wished for her. I am determined that she shall have it."

He nodded his head. "Fair enough, Mr. Darcy. I shouldn't be surprised if I did the same, were I in your shoes. Perhaps I might renew my friendship with her at a later time." He bowed and withdrew.

Darcy rested his elbows on the desk and steepled his fingers. Mr. Sutherland seemed a respectable man. The fault with this situation lay with Lady Catherine, who had improperly encouraged him. Was she trying to punish Darcy for marrying Elizabeth? But that did not seem like her.

A scratch at the door was followed by Georgiana's entrance. She looked more and more like their mother as Darcy remembered her; graceful and tall, smooth dark hair, wide brown eyes.

"Did he offer for me?" Georgiana asked quietly.

Darcy was relieved to see that she was not upset. After the Ramsgate affair, he had been very afraid that any man who made up to her would terrify her.

"Not quite, but he got mighty near it."

"I thought he might."

"Would you have wanted me to accept?" Darcy asked, surprised by her slightly melancholy tone.

She laughed, though still a little sadly. "No. I would not!"

"Good. You are far too young. I insist that you see a little more of the world before making a decision of this magnitude."

She trailed her fingers over the desk. "See a little more of the world," she echoed.

"Is it true that my aunt has been encouraging him?"

"Well, it is either that or else she felt it imperative that he teach me whist."

Darcy put his hand on hers. "I am sorry, Georgiana."

"It is fine. Honestly, I did spend more time with him the last few days, of my own free will. He is unexacting and affable; I suppose I could do worse."

"You could also do much better. If you are trying to make me feel better, you are failing. What you truly mean is that you were so starved for decent companionship you turned to him in default."

She winced and Darcy felt like a complete failure. He should not have allowed her to make this sacrifice, no matter how resolute she'd been or how expedient the solution. But there was no use repining over past decisions.

"We shall go to the London house while I finish up some business I must attend to," he said instead. "And the second week in July we will go on to Hertfordshire, to stay at Netherfield with Bingley until the wedding."

"Oh. We would not stay with the Bennets? Is that not done with the bride's family?"

"It sometimes is… but we will be more comfortable at Netherfield." Darcy was trying to behave with the utmost consideration for Lizzy's family, but the truth was that they wore him down. With the best will in the world to think well of them, they still often startled him with their carelessness, impropriety, or sheer volume.

It was a little better with the youngest daughter away—though that was another piece of mismanagement, in his opinion—but still not at all what Georgiana was used to.

He, who had never shirked any difficult task, could not wait for August when the engagement would be behind him. Then he could return to Pemberley with Elizabeth and Georgiana. What paradise!

He enjoyed being engaged to Elizabeth; it was excessively better than *not* being engaged to her. Only... they did not actually have very much time together. And when they were alone, she was not...

Well, he could not criticize. He had pictured perhaps something more spontaneous and informal, but it was as if, unless he was mistaken, she grew more proper every day. Stiffer with him rather than less. He did not know if he was the cause of it, and if so, how to undo it.

"By the by," he said, "I want to get a portrait of Elizabeth, to hang in the gallery at Pemberley. What do you think of this man Lady Catherine employed to paint Anne?"

Georgiana nearly laughed. What did she think of him? She thought he was kind, talented, and...

She shook her head to clear it.

"No good?" he asked.

"No, no, he's quite good. Anne's portrait is all but complete."

"I shall have a look at it then. I still don't know that anyone could do justice to Elizabeth's eyes," he said with a smile, "but it is worth the attempt."

Georgiana smiled, but her heart raced. If she encouraged her brother to hire Mr. Turner, it would probably happen. Then Mr. Turner might come to Pemberley! But she immediately recognized the foolishness of this. It would change nothing. It would be to taunt herself with what could never be.

"You shall have to judge his work for yourself," Georgiana said. "I cannot advise you."

9

JOHN WAS MORE THAN A LITTLE interested to meet Miss Darcy's brother.

John had been absent from the drawing room when Mr. Darcy was announced, but he was present when Mr. Darcy returned from his brief conversation with Mr. Sutherland. John could easily guess what *that* had been about. Mr. Sutherland's face was not noticeably cast down, but he shared a brief look with Lady Catherine and shook his head.

John felt insensibly cheered.

Mr. Darcy was polite to his aunt and did not bring the matter up, but John suspected, from a certain militant look in the man's eyes, that he would take his aunt to task for this piece of meddling.

Good. John wanted to know there was someone in Miss Darcy's life who would stand up for her.

He was a little surprised when Mr. Darcy also asked to see the portrait of Anne.

Mr. Darcy explained, "I am getting married next month. I want to have a portrait made of my wife for the gallery at Pemberley." The explanation was for John, but the clipped words seemed directed at Lady Catherine, rather like knives.

She took a sharp breath, and her fingers curled into claws on the armrests.

"Of course," John said quickly. "In the library."

Mr. Darcy held out a hand for his sister. "You must help me, Georgiana. You are much more artistic than I. You would know what Elizabeth would like."

Miss de Bourgh's portrait was complete except for a few finishing touches, and John had given her as much natural expression as he could muster while still making her look essentially like herself.

Georgiana had not been here during the last sitting, the only one she had missed, and she exclaimed over the painting now. "You did capture a smile! Did you ask her about the races?"

"I tried, but apparently the magic was gone. This was from our ride through the fields the other day."

"She did enjoy that ride, but I thought you were only lost in thought," Georgiana said.

John couldn't help the pleasure he felt to have her speaking freely to him again. "Only in part, I was also fixing that image in my mind."

Mr. Darcy gestured at the painting and the ornate gold frame waiting nearby. "It's very good, but I don't know if Elizabeth would like something like this."

Georgiana bit her lip. "Perhaps a miniature, instead? Oh, and you could have another made to give to her family as a wedding gift. I'm sure they would appreciate that, as they are, in a sense, losing her to us."

Mr. Darcy tilted his head. "Miniatures are watercolor though, yes? I think it would look rather washed out amongst our forebears."

John agreed. "Unless you have a section of the gallery dedicated to watercolor, it might not quite fit. I might suggest a *demi poire* instead."

"A— half pear?" Georgiana translated.

"It's popular in France just now. Larger than a miniature, about so," he formed a rectangle with his hands. "Done in oils, often three-quarter face, thought that's a matter of taste. Dark, simple background. A little less than a bust, a little more than a miniature…"

"How long does it take?" Darcy asked.

"One or two sittings is usually sufficient, and only a week or two to complete. Many families do them when their son or husband is going to war or daughter getting married. Things of that sort."

But what was he saying? Did he want to spend more time with Georgiana? He must be crazy.

Miss Darcy had been very embarrassed after their conversation over her portfolio. He was a little afraid that she had seen something in his face that upset her. She had hardly looked him in the eye since, and he could count on one hand the number of things she'd said to him.

Her avoidance had both relieved and perturbed him. Perturbed because not seeing her made his days dull and empty, relieved because he knew he ought not indulge any such affection for her, and her avoidance of *him* relieved him of the duty of avoiding *her*. He really ought not prolong their acquaintance. But on the other hand, he was not so beforehand with the world as to be turning down lucrative offers.

"I like that idea." Mr. Darcy nodded his head. "Would you be available in July? Meryton is much closer to London than Pemberley."

"I'm not familiar with Meryton."

"Due east of Watford, a few miles."

John gave up, feeling both guilty and elated. "During the first half of July I will be a guest of Mrs. Winkleigh; she desires a bust painting of her son. Would the second half of July suit? Say the 17th? I believe Miss Darcy told me the wedding was not until the last of the month, which would allow adequate time."

"Capital," Darcy said. "I will give you the address and direction for Netherfield, where we can easily lodge you."

"Thank you, sir." John couldn't help trying to read Miss Darcy's expression. Did she mind seeing him again? Was she indifferent? Was she perhaps glad?

Georgiana turned away. "When do we depart?"

She and her brother exited the library together and John remained behind. He absently ghosted his fingers over the frame.

He would like to paint Miss Darcy someday. He would paint her at the piano, in her favorite white shawl that she wore so often when she was sick. She would be in profile, and only the slight uplift of her cheek would show that she was happy. He rather thought a small dog or cat ought to be in the picture too, because she would enjoy that. And, in his mind, there would also be a fond husband standing behind her, perhaps turning a page of the music with his paint-stained fingers.

"I am an idiot," John muttered. "And no one to blame but myself."

Georgiana planned to say her farewells to everyone that evening, as Darcy wanted to get an early start. They were only going to London, so an early start was not technically necessary, but he did not want to stay under Lady Catherine's roof any longer than he must. At least not at present.

The Collinses had been invited for dinner, and Georgiana bid a rather warmer goodbye to Mrs. Collins.

That lady squeezed Georgiana's hands and said quietly, "I do not know if I shall make it to the wedding. My husband is… he and Lady Catherine are still not accustomed to the idea. Please let Lizzy know that I would not miss it for the world, were it possible to come."

Mrs. Collins had always a calm, practical air, but this time her eyes were suspiciously bright.

"Of course," Georgiana said. "I will tell her. Perhaps we could hire a carriage—"

"No, no. That's not your responsibility. I daresay my father might send a coach for me if I asked, or I could travel on the mail. But... but *if* I should not be able to come, I shall be happy to know that she is gaining such a good sister."

"Thank you!"

Georgiana's farewell to Mr. Turner was limited, which was probably good. He shook her hand, as was commonly done in some circles, and wished her adieu. "I look forward to officially meeting your sister-in-law when I see you next."

Georgiana smiled and nodded. She hoped very much that this giddy excitement she felt would be under firm control by then.

{ 10 }

WHEN GEORGIANA AND HER BROTHER arrived at Netherfield nearly a week later, Lizzy was on hand to greet them. Georgiana was very thankful. Otherwise it would only have been Caroline Bingley and Caroline's sister, Louisa Hurst, and that would have been very dismal indeed.

Lizzy barely waited for Georgiana to alight from the carriage before embracing her, and Georgiana felt tears of relief prick her eyes. Rosings had not been overfull of friendly faces.

"You are finally here," Lizzy said. "I am so happy. Truly, I've been lying awake nights thinking of you; I could not have been more concerned if I had a brother in action on the Continent."

Lizzy released her to greet Darcy. Georgiana loved the look on his face, the deeply satisfied, all-was-right-with-the-world look. He brought Lizzy's hand up and kissed it, and almost, she was sure, meant to kiss Lizzy on the lips.

That would have been perhaps a little forward, but they *were* engaged. At the last second, he seemed to reconsider, and only nodded, rather formally. Georgiana was disappointed.

Lizzy did not seem surprised, though, and only a slight slump to her shoulders made Georgiana think she also was disappointed. She turned back to Georgiana. "I won't tease you further, for Darcy looks quite serious. Let me take you up instead. I know Caroline will think it odd if you do not come up to them at once, and then I can introduce you to my sister. I know you met in passing at the Wells, but now you have time to get really acquainted."

"My dear Miss Darcy." Caroline embraced Georgiana warmly when they reached the drawing room. "I am ever so pleased to see you. You must tell me if everything in your room is not quite to your liking. I have quite missed you since we returned from Tunbridge. I have told Louisa, 'We shall have our sweet young friend with us again soon.' I assure you, we miss you prodigiously."

"Thank you," Georgiana said.

Jane's greeting was more reticent and less caressing, but when she told Georgiana how happy she and Lizzy were to gain her as a sister, her eyes shone with sincerity.

Between them, Jane and Mr. Bingley and Lizzy were a merry, cheerful group. Darcy was still a bit quiet, perhaps still angry about Lady Catherine's attempted matchmaking, but even he could not stay grave and silent when he was with Lizzy.

Caroline was languid and haughty with the others, but her manner changed quite markedly whenever she spoke to Georgiana, becoming soft and kind. It was too marked to be less than awkward. Georgiana had never understood Caroline's caressing manner, feeling that Caroline did not particularly know or like her, and she understood it even less now.

Thankfully, Georgiana discovered she was less intimidated by the worldly, fashionable Caroline than she had used to be. Perhaps staying at Rosings had taught her a certain amount of resilience. Or perhaps it was Lizzy's influence.

Either way, when Caroline escorted Georgiana to the room prepared for her and attempted to commiserate with Georgiana on the "coming nuptials," Georgiana's chin rose.

"I cannot imagine a better match for my brother. They are extremely well-suited." She turned to look at the room and asked brightly, "Is this the bell-pull? I shall ring for my maid."

The next afternoon Georgiana rode with Mr. Bingley in his phaeton to pay a visit on the Bennet family. Darcy begged off, declaring that he simply must look over the latest questions sent to him by his bailiff and reply as soon as may be.

Georgiana could tell at once that these visits to Longbourn were no longer a matter of ceremony, for Lizzy greeted them at the door rather than waiting for them to be announced. Furthermore, Mrs. Bennet and Miss Kitty didn't lead her properly to the sitting room, but greeted her with boisterous exclamations. They invited Georgiana to join them in the morning room, which seemed to be covered with sewing projects.

Mrs. Bennet did *begin* to have a chat with Georgiana, but she was quickly distracted by Kitty who was sorting a quantity of silk flowers. This led to an argument about bonnets, which led to both of them quitting the room. Mrs. Bennet threw an apology towards Georgiana and Mrs. Annesley as she left the room, still declaring that she knew exactly the bonnet she meant—how could Kitty be stupid enough to think it had been thrown out?—and she would be back directly.

Georgiana smiled as Mrs. Bennet excused herself, but she did feel a trifle awkward to be left alone with only Mrs. Annesley. Should she go out or wait here? Jane and Mr. Bingley had gone on a brief walk, and Lizzy had been called away by their housekeeper to settle some dispute.

They sat in silence for a moment.

"This is a nice, homely room," Mrs. Annesley said eventually. "Very comfortable."

"Yes." Georgiana was far from being offended, but she did not quite know how to behave on such a casual visit. Ordinarily she would never go wandering around someone's house or grounds, but… "Shall we—go out into the garden?"

Mrs. Annesley looked similarly conflicted. "I am sure Mrs. Bennet will return soon."

Thankfully, Lizzy's middle sister, Mary, entered only a few minutes later. But Mary seemed startled to see them sitting quietly and alone. She did enter and sit, but she seemed very ill at ease.

"I—I see you are all very busy with wedding clothes," Georgiana said.

Mary's lips pursed. "I do not approve of much finery; but I understand the cultural reverence for matrimony demands it."

"Oh. I suppose." Georgiana wracked her mind. Wedding finery was not a good topic. She was formulating a question on Mary's interests when Mary spoke up.

"I am reading a very interesting book about Christian martyrs, by Mr. Foxe. Did you know that at times the Catholic executioners would stuff a man's mouth with gunpowder so that his head would explode?"

"Oh. Oh my. I have heard of the book, but never read—"

"Every good Protestant should read it," Mary said decidedly. "Such affecting examples of patience in affliction and death. Did you know that a red-hot poker would be used to pull out the finger and toenails, and sometimes to drive a hole through the accused's hands?"

Georgiana could not help grimacing.

"Yes, an excellent book," Mrs. Annesley said. "I have read it several times; however, I am not sure the tortures it describes are an appropriate topic of conversation."

Mary nodded, but looked a little sullen. "Please excuse me," she said after a moment, quitting the room abruptly.

Georgiana turned helplessly to Mrs. Annesley. "Should I have tried something else?"

Mrs. Annesley's brow was furrowed. "Perhaps when she returns… I—I daresay she thought of something that needed her attention."

They sat in silence rather longer than the first time, occasionally hearing the voice of Mrs. Bennet calling or footsteps passing by. Georgiana squirmed.

She was beyond relieved when Jane and Mr. Bingley entered.

"Oh! Miss Darcy," Jane exclaimed. "I just passed Mama in the dining room and thought you must be with Mary in the music room. Your brother tells us you love the pianoforte."

Georgiana smiled uncertainly. "I do. I—I wasn't certain where she was."

Jane immediately gathered what had happened and her face showed mortification. "I am so sorry! My mama is very distracted, but we should not have left you. Would you care for a tour of Longbourn, such as it is?"

Georgiana willingly agreed. She found Longbourn charming, because as Lizzy's home, it could not be otherwise. She couldn't help feeling, at the same time, that it was a bit… worn, and the family areas were rather… full. But then with five daughters, how else should it look?

Jane was sweet and kind, but she was reserved, and as Georgiana was not a talker herself, they did not make much progress in getting to know one another. If asked, however, they would both have proclaimed their immediate and undying affection for the other.

Georgiana was relieved when Lizzy reappeared at their sides.

Jane turned. "There you are. I am afraid Miss Darcy has been rather overlooked this afternoon!"

Lizzy winced. "Oh no! I ought to have stayed nearby. Please forgive us, Miss Darcy. We have never had even one wedding in the family, and now we are to have two!"

Georgiana smiled warmly. "I am sure it is most taxing! Please don't give it another thought."

Mr. Bingley took Georgiana's arm. "That's a good girl. I suppose it is time we returned to Netherfield."

Mrs. Bennet was just joining them. "But I quite counted on Miss Darcy and yourself taking sup with us!"

"Not today, ma'am. Told Darcy and my sisters I'd bring Georgie home for dinner. Otherwise, I would stay. You know I stand on no ceremony with you."

Mrs. Bennet swatted his arm playfully. "As if I didn't know. You have positively haunted the place for the last month and I don't know when Jane has been happier. I knew she couldn't have been so beautiful for nothing!"

The next morning, feeling that he had executed as much business as he could until the next missive from his bailiff, Darcy took Georgiana for a drive. She had not seen much of Hertfordshire as yet. He positioned the whip, twitched the reins, and the horses pulled them down the long drive toward the lane. "I don't think I have ever experienced such an interminable June and July. They have lasted at least twenty weeks already," Darcy said.

Georgiana smiled. "You are eager to be married."

"Yes. Well, not only that, but also to be back at Pemberley. I made a flying trip there while you were at Rosings, but when I left last winter I never intended to be gone for planting. At least I shall be back by harvest."

"You are not going on a wedding trip?"

He shook his head. "I asked Elizabeth if we might postpone it, due to my long absence from home."

"Oh. We will all return to Pemberley directly after the wedding?"

He coughed. "I wanted to ask you about that. Would you mind terribly if Elizabeth and I spent a few weeks alone at Pemberley, before you return?"

"Of- of course not."

"Bingley and Jane will be visiting us after their own short wedding trip to Portsmouth. You could travel up with them."

He tried to study Georgiana's face. A bride or groom's sister was often included in wedding trips, but he wanted to have Elizabeth to himself. He loved Georgiana very much, but he wanted Elizabeth's conversation and attention without distraction. He felt there was still some… distance between them. He could not account for it, because she was always sweet and sometimes playful, and he was very much in love with her… and yet still there was a sort of formality that lay between them.

It was self-indulgent, but he wanted the time alone. Were it at anyone other than Georgiana's expense, he would not have felt so guilty.

She raised her head. "Of course, you should do so. How pleasant and quiet it will be for the two of you after these last weeks of bustle."

"Thank you."

"But I think… Would it be possible for me to stay with the Bennets for the interim after the wedding?"

Darcy frowned. He was doing his best to like Elizabeth's family, but while he could recognize their affection and essential decency, there was a haphazardness to their life he could not like. Their home and lifestyles were characterized by inattention and overindulgence.

"The Bennets are very kind, but they do not lead the sort of life you are used to. Miss Bingley…." He trailed off.

"I know the Bennets are… are quite informal and perhaps… loud," Georgiana stumbled. "And Caroline and Louisa are very fine, but I would still infinitely rather stay with the Bennets."

Darcy did not like it, but it did not seem fair to leave her behind and deny her the choice of residence. "Let me consider, please."

Georgiana nodded. "Did you tell Lizzy about the portraits?"

"Ah. Yes, I did. She said it was extravagant but that it would please her mother enormously. She said her mother's friends will admire it and her mother will reply with a sigh, 'My daughter, Mrs. Darcy!'"

Georgiana laughed. "I am glad."

"As am I. Furthermore, the portraits are a good reason to have Elizabeth more at Netherfield, since that's where the artist fellow will be staying. I must remind Caroline to make up a room for him on the 17th."

{ 11 }

JOHN'S ARRIVAL AT NETHERFIELD was quiet, as he had hoped. He arrived in the mid-afternoon, when the family might reasonably be out visiting, walking, or riding, and he timed it well, for only one lady was at home, a Miss Bingley.

She did not seem terribly pleased about his presence but gave orders for him to be shown to his room.

Perhaps Lady Catherine was not the only one unhappy about Mr. Darcy's marriage. It was a salutary reminder to John. Darcy's circle was reluctant to accept Miss Elizabeth Bennet, who was unexceptionable as far as he could discover, except for not having a large fortune. How much more would they reject a man such as John Turner for Miss Darcy!

The family returned for dinner and John somewhat anxiously prepared for it. He always dressed for dinner when staying in places such as this, though his clothes were still plain. It was a compromise between the plain dress he considered appropriate and the formality considered appropriate by his patrons and clients.

He found the butler and requested that a message be taken to the kitchens that he would prefer water to be served to him at dinner.

The butler looked at him askance. Servants often reacted as though he'd asked for the master's best brandy instead of merely water.

John squared his shoulders and raised his eyebrows.

"Very good, sir," the butler said reluctantly.

When John entered the parlor where he was told the family gathered before dinner, only Mr. Darcy was present.

"Ah. Turner, I heard you were arrived." Mr. Darcy rose to shake his hand. "I took the initiative to plan for my fiancée to wait on you tomorrow morning."

"Thank you, sir, that will work perfectly."

Mr. Darcy sat down and opened a newspaper, so John suited himself to his company and sat down with a book he found on the coffee table.

"I say, am I being rude?" Mr. Darcy asked, putting down his newspaper. "I don't mean to ignore you, only I have had enough chatter for ten men." He spoke ruefully, not at all as if he looked down on John, but rather invited him to understand.

John responded at once. "Not at all. I am the eldest of seven and have two sisters married. Enjoy the silence while you can."

"Exactly. Thank you."

They sat in mutual quiet and satisfaction until the rest of the party arrived.

Georgiana waited until the last moment to descend for dinner. She both desired and dreaded a solo conversation with Mr. Turner.

With the room full of Bingleys, Hursts, and Darcys, he greeted her with a bow. "Miss Darcy."

She curtseyed. "Mr. Turner."

It was a little harder to sit across from him at dinner. Even worse, he was largely ignored by the others.

Over the second course, however, Mr. Bingley began to question him about his work, and Louisa perked up at the mention of some of his former subjects.

Mr. Bingley snapped his fingers. "I must have you paint Jane while you're here."

Caroline sniffed. "I'm sure he wouldn't have enough time, Charles. The wedding is less than two weeks away and he's already doing two *demi poire* of Miss Elizabeth."

"I could probably do one more, in addition to the two portraits of Miss Elizabeth," Mr. Turner said. "These paintings are much less taxing, as they are smaller, and the background is less elaborate, usually dark. Much of the time is spent waiting for the paint to dry; multiple pieces do not take much longer than the first."

"Wonderful!" Bingley said. "You see, Darcy, sometimes my impetuous ideas are not so far-fetched."

Darcy raised his brows. "I did not say anything."

"You were thinking it. I could tell."

Mr. Turner took a sip from his glass and Bingley fixated on it.

"I say, what's that you're drinking? Can I offer you some of this red? Or the Madeira?"

"No, thank you, I am fine."

Bingley looked concerned and Mr. Turner smiled. "I'm a Methodist, you see. Though not a very good one at present, I haven't been to a class meeting in a month."

Georgiana returned his smile without meaning to.

Darcy leaned forward. "Yes, we have a congregation at Lambton, led by a Mr. Johnson. Not enough of a group for an elder, I was told. I was afraid there might be some conflict, but they seem to be a conscientious, community-minded group."

Mr. Turner inclined his head.

Mr. Hurst wiped his mouth. "It's spreading like wildfire in Yorkshire. Workers like hearing that they're better than the gentry."

Mr. Turner sipped his water again. "Not better, sir, only equal in the eyes of God."

Caroline tipped her head. "Doesn't every church teach as much? However, equality in the eyes of God does not mean that everyone is of the same station or class. God places some above others."

Mr. Turner looked as if he might answer but met Georgiana's eye and instead only smiled politely at Caroline.

Georgiana did not like any kind of conflict.

"I think it is strange," Louisa chimed in, "how you will meet with Baptists, Quakers, Methodists, and Scotch Calvinists everywhere these days... My father says England will end as republican as the former colonies if we do not address it."

This time Mr. Turner did answer. "I cannot speak for all Protestant sects, of course, but I have no political ambitions that would worry the Prime Minister. Methodism encourages all energy and zeal to be poured into spiritual pursuits, not revolution."

Mr. Hurst scoffed. "Him! Shouldn't wonder if our dear Mr. Perceval was a closet Methodist himself. Prime Minister, indeed."

The debate continued and Georgiana even ventured a question or two. But she was relieved when the ladies retired from the table and the conversation was broken up.

{ 12 }

I N THE MORNING, GEORGIANA accompanied Lizzy to the rear parlor, which had been converted to a painting studio for Mr. Turner. He'd said he only needed good light and space for his easel, so Miss Bingley had judged this to be the best room for the use.

Georgiana suspected Miss Bingley chose it because it was small and out of the way of the rest of the house, being nearly tucked away behind the secondary stair that the servants used.

But it did have good light, being on the corner of the second floor, with a large gable window on one side and two high, smallish windows on the next. Perhaps Georgiana was judging Miss Bingley too harshly.

Lizzy greeted Mr. Turner with a warm smile. "My good friend Mrs. Collins has told me nothing but good things of you."

"Ah. My long-suffering whist partner! Please send my regards to Mrs. Collins when you next write her."

"I will. Shall I sit here in the window seat? I warn you that my expectations are high and if I am not ravishingly beautiful in my portrait, I shall wish to know why." She fluttered her eyelashes.

Mr. Turner laughed. "I see you shall not need to be flattered, ma'am."

"Do your subjects generally need praise? I cannot blame them. I myself am full of confidence, but even I feel the awkwardness in having an artist study your features."

Lizzy displayed no actual awkwardness, and Mr. Turner chuckled as he began to sketch. "I do not usually tell my sitters this; but the truth is that often while painting I am so focused on detail and faithful reproduction that you might as well be an urn or a piece of fruit as far as my thoughts."

Lizzy laughed. "That *does* put me at my ease."

He glanced back and forth as he continued to sketch. "I believe I shall have the privilege of painting your elder sister as well."

"Yes. Dear Jane! She is very modest, so you might have to put her at ease, but she is by far the prettiest Bennet, so that should make your job easier."

He smiled. "Believe it or not, beauty does not actually aid the portraitist. If you paint a plain woman passably well, her family is pleased. But if you paint a beautiful woman one jot less beautiful than they perceive, you have utterly failed to capture her likeness."

Lizzy tapped her chin. "That is a problem. So, you would rather paint the plain?"

He shook his head. "Perhaps I misspoke. I don't think I have ever painted anyone truly plain. Every face is interesting, and some of those perceived to be lesser have had the more interesting characteristics! But I have painted people whose family *perceived* them as plain, and the reverse."

"How diplomatic. You have quite the unique opportunity to observe a variety of people. I suppose a good portraitist must also be a studier of human nature."

He assented, but lapsed into silence again, quickly delineating the outline of Lizzy's face and hair, and then lightly putting in the shape of brow, eyes, and nose. Georgiana had drifted behind and to the left, where she could watch the picture take shape.

Lizzy sat obediently still for a while, but often shifted one ankle behind the other, rubbed her lip, or sighed. "I have never excelled at sitting quietly," she commented.

"I am not a good conversationalist while I work, but you may certainly talk to Miss Darcy," he said. "I shall let you know if I need you to be entirely still."

Lizzy cocked her head. "I will only ask you one more question, sir. Do you think you could paint four such portraits in the allotted time, rather than three?"

He laughed. "Perhaps, but I fear if I agree there will be still more. Do you not have four sisters, ma'am? Then there would be Miss Bingley and Mrs. Hurst to be included." He hesitated. "And Miss Darcy would make seven."

Elizabeth laughed merrily. "I swear I shall not require seven portraits of you, Mr. Turner! I only want the last on your list, Miss Darcy. Then we will hang them both in Pemberley and my poor portrait will not feel so strange and alone in whatever great gallery it is put. The other portraits would not dare disdain me if a true Darcy is there by my side to defend me."

Georgiana shook her head at once. "No, no. You are funning, I know, but you do not need a portrait of me."

"People seldom *need* portraits, Georgiana, they only want them," Lizzy argued. "I suppose I am already learning to be extravagant, but I would love to have one of you done at the same time as mine, in the same style, to commemorate my first year as part of your family."

"My brother should have his done, in that case."

"I tried." Lizzy sighed dramatically. "He assures me there is a recent portrait of his already hanging in the gallery and that he will feel a popinjay if he has to see another of his likenesses there until he is quite old."

"Oh, that's true," Georgiana reflected. "It was more than seven years ago, but he does not look so very different."

"Then it must be you! If Mr. Turner feels he can add to his workload?"

There was another slight hesitation, which might have been accounted for by his absorption in squeezing out dark paint onto a palette. "Yes, I believe so."

"Excellent!"

Mr. Turner looked over his shoulder at Georgiana, and she tried to look serene, but was afraid her discomfort was visible.

He cleared his throat. "Perhaps you could sit this afternoon, say at one? After I have blocked in Miss Elizabeth's portrait, I will have leisure to begin yours."

Lizzy answered for her. "Yes, that will work. My sister is paying calls with our mother today, so she will not wait on you until tomorrow."

Georgiana assented weakly.

Lizzy's eyes twinkled at her. "Come, I should be so cast down if we didn't have it. Someday far in the future when you visit Pemberley, I will be able to point it out to my children. 'Yes, there is Aunt Georgiana's picture—or shall we perhaps call you Aunt Georgie? I feel there shall be a nickname!—there is Aunt Georgie's picture from the year I met her.' And they shall exclaim at how much you look like your daughter, or some such thing. Then we shall both feel old and wise and tell them how quickly the time passes." She laughed. "Oh dear. I have just made myself melancholy without in the least meaning to."

Georgiana couldn't help laughing at Lizzy's woeful tone. "It serves you right for using guilt to make me agree with you."

Lizzy dimpled. "Oh no. You have already agreed to oblige me, I am only using guilt to make you enjoy it."

{ 13 }

JOHN WAS STILL IN THE REAR PARLOR some hours later when Georgiana and Miss Elizabeth returned for Georgiana's sitting. He'd set the smallish canvas with Miss Elizabeth's outline and preliminary blocking upright against the wall next to him. A newly prepared canvas was on the easel for Georgiana. He'd previously covered the Persian rug for its protection.

Miss Elizabeth had the air of one who was frog-marching a subordinate to their doom. "I have assured her I shall keep her company, but if she darts for the door, I might need to restrain her."

Georgiana protested, "I am not—"

"And no lock on the door, how provoking!"

Georgiana's cheeks were turning a mottled red and Miss Elizabeth sobered. "I am sorry; my tongue gets away from me. I am in the habit of teasing my sisters and forget that you are not in that habit."

"It's fine," she murmured.

"Take a seat, Miss Darcy," John said, as reassuringly as he could muster. "And I will keep you as short a time as possible."

Elizabeth positioned herself as Georgiana had done this morning so that she could see him lay down the first sketch. She succeeded in engaging Georgiana in conversation—something about after-wedding plans with the Bennets—so John was able to sketch in peace.

He was so focused, he noticed when a bead of sweat appeared on Georgiana's forehead. It was not an overly warm day for July.

"Are you feeling well, Miss Darcy?" he asked.

"Fine." She touched her forehead, surreptitiously removing the sign of stress.

Elizabeth peered a little closer at his drawing. "That is already *very* like her. I think it is better than mine—more like, I mean. Did you sketch Georgiana at Rosings?"

"No. Why would I—" He fumbled with his pencil and dropped it. "No, this is the first time I have sketched Miss Darcy." He leaned over and hoped that would account for a slightly reddened face. It was true that he had never sketched her, but he had given too much thought to her. Her face came to his pencil almost as easily as a self-portrait, which he'd done many times in practice.

Lizzy stepped out of his way so he might retrieve the pencil. A sudden suspicion had occurred to her. "It is only that you sketch so confidently, I suppose. It gives the impression of familiarity."

She fell silent, looking between Mr. Turner and Georgiana.

Lizzy had easily attributed Georgiana's reluctance to be painted to her reserved and shy nature, but perhaps it was not that but Mr. Turner himself. He, whom Lizzy had immediately judged to be a good-natured, confident young man, had just displayed something very like guilt on being asked whether he had sketched Miss Darcy.

Lizzy's first protective thought, that Georgiana was uncomfortable because of unwanted attention from Mr. Turner, was almost immediately dismissed. Poor Georgiana had already been the victim of an improper attempted seduction; surely she would tell her brother if something of a similar nature happened again so soon! Nor did Mr. Turner's character, even on slight acquaintance, seem the type.

No, if there was anything here—Lizzy was no longer so confident in her judgments as she used to be!—it was more likely a genuine partiality on his part.

Lizzy hoped it was not so, for both their sakes. From the way he spoke and a few comments he'd made about his family, she was fairly certain he hailed from the middle class. His parents were apparently wealthy enough to send him to a good school and he had been sponsored into the Royal Art Academy, but they were not landowners, not gentry. His work brought him into the Darcy's circle, and he had taken steps to fit in, but he was not a "gentleman-born."

It strained her imagination to picture Mr. Darcy approving such a relationship in any fashion. True, he had apologized multiple times for his arrogance and superiority on first meeting her. Also true, he was dealing with her mother's occasional unbecoming behavior with restraint, if not with grace. But at least Mr. Bennet was a gentleman!

Lizzy observed them both closely, while continuing to chatter about various topics as they came to mind—Mr. Turner would think her tongue ran on wheels!—and Lizzy tentatively concluded that the affection was mutual. Georgiana was not a master of controlling her expressions, and when Mr. Turner was not looking at her, her face occasionally grew wistful, even admiring.

When he *was* looking at her—well, perhaps he generally looked at portrait subjects as if they were urns or apples, but he was not looking at Georgiana that way. There was a small smile around his mouth, wiped away when he thought about it. When they made eye contact, Lizzy was not sure who was at more pains to look away first. Miss Darcy seemed to find the wall behind their heads very interesting, and of course Mr. Turner always had the excuse of his canvas.

Lizzy was dismayed, a most unusual sensation for her. She had only known Georgiana for a few months but was already well on the way to loving her like a sister. If Georgiana truly fell in love with Mr. Turner…

But they did not know each other well enough for that! Did they?

Lizzy herself was given to quick prejudices and partialities, and only witness how that had misled her! But Georgiana was nothing like Lizzy. Furthermore, Georgiana had spent nearly a month with him at Rosings… many a debutante had to commit her future to a man she knew far less well.

Not that Mr. Darcy would force his sister into marriage with a veritable stranger; that fate did not await Georgiana. But neither would Darcy, unless Lizzy was much mistaken, think Mr. Turner even remotely eligible. He had unbent amazingly after Lizzy's rebuke of his behavior in Hertfordshire, but he was still prone to certain kinds of pride.

And no one would blame him for rejecting such a man such as Mr. Turner for Miss Darcy. All of polite society would declare it a scandal for Miss Darcy, an heiress who was not even out, to contract an engagement with a relatively unknown portrait artist.

Lizzy could only hope that it was a passing fancy. But the brightness of Georgiana's eyes and the stilted nature of their conversation as he finished his sketch did nothing to encourage her.

{ 14 }

GEORGIANA WAS BOTH GLAD and unhappy to leave Mr. Turner to his work. She was not exactly comfortable being with him—certainly not with him staring at her, as he must!—but she found being apart from him sadly flat.

"Would you care for a stroll in the garden before I return home?" Lizzy asked. "Tomorrow my youngest sister, Lydia, returns from Brighton, so I will not have as many moments for quiet conversation hereafter."

They both retrieved their shawls and Mrs. Annesley accompanied them out to the garden. Her ankle was much better from the sprain it had received in the Wells, but she was looking tired, and when the girls pressed her to sit in the sun by the fountain and rest, she was quite willing to do so.

Lizzy walked rather faster than Georgiana was accustomed to, but Georgiana was the taller one, so she soon lengthened her stride and became comfortable. Georgiana and her brother inherited their height from their grandfather, and while it was an asset for a gentleman, not so for a lady. At least not a lady like Georgiana.

"You ought to be tall," Georgiana said.

"Without a doubt," Lizzy agreed, at once. "I wonder no one has mentioned it before."

Georgiana giggled.

"Is there any particular reason I ought to be tall?"

"People expect tall girls to be social and witty and... and poised. I am not any of those things, but *you* are. If I could trade my size for yours, I think it would be more fitting." Georgiana had never spoken of this so bluntly with anyone and rather thought she might have broken a social rule. "I apologize. I know I ought not to complain."

Lizzy patted her arm. "You are only expressing a feeling; you don't have to apologize for that."

"Well, I know that God makes us, and we ought not grumble about what he has done."

"Please tell my sisters that. They seem to think that anything worth noticing is worth complaining about. Yesterday it was each other."

"Even Jane? I would not think...."

Lizzy laughed. "No, Jane never whines or grumbles, but I am not sure that is spiritual discipline or sheer inability to think two negative thoughts in a row."

"I think she and Mr. Bingley will deal extremely," Georgiana said, tentatively. "I do not know either of them very well, but they seem of a similar joyful temperament."

"They are; I believe you are right. And your brother and I are of a similar prickly disposition, and so we shall either deal well or poke each other to death."

Georgiana's eyes widened. "Oh no, I would not describe either of you that way."

"I am only funning. I want you to know, by the by, that I quite view you as our matchmaker. I had begun to move beyond my first prejudiced impression of your brother, but it was your sweet disposition and praise of him that truly encouraged me to think of him differently."

Georgiana blushed. "I know I was very forward, considering our slight acquaintance at the time; but he was so very unhappy."

"You were not too forward; you were everything a good sister ought to be."

"Thank you. Now that I know how it feels to be on the receiving end of… of that sort of interference… I was rather ashamed of myself."

"Wait—the receiving end…? Do you mean matchmaking?"

Georgiana was confused. "With Mr. Sutherland? Did my brother not tell you?"

"No! Who is this Mr. Sutherland?"

"He is a neighbor of my Aunt de Bourgh. I'm afraid she encouraged him and… and he offered for me."

"Oh, dear. Did he speak to you or…"

"Oh no. That would be very improper, would it not? He spoke with my brother."

Lizzy smiled a little and Georgiana suddenly recollected that Darcy had proposed to Elizabeth and not spoken to her father first. "Not improper! I did not mean to say…"

"Do not worry! To tell the truth, I think in less exalted circles it is more acceptable to speak with the lady in question and ascertain her feelings before speaking with her guardian."

"Oh."

"I am only sorry that you should have been teased with this while you were at Rosings! You wrote nothing of it. I don't think you even mentioned Mr. Sutherland by name."

"I was not happy about the situation, but it did not… I was not greatly troubled by it."

Lizzy looked searchingly at her. "Were you not?"

Georgiana worried her lip. The truth, she suspected, was that she would have been *very* troubled by it, were it not for the superior distraction of Mr. Turner. She was too troubled by her growing feelings for him to be disturbed by the calm Mr. Sutherland.

"I suppose I didn't find him offensive or… or overbearing," she offered eventually.

"Did you perhaps feel a partiality for him?" Lizzy asked. "That can render a man much less odious."

"No, that I did not."

"It would be acceptable if you had, you know. You are allowed to feel a partiality."

Georgiana felt rather brazen. Did sisters talk about such things so openly? What if someone heard them?

Lizzy paused, then continued. "I am not always wise; I only want you to know that you are allowed to have feelings. Mr. Darcy says we will take you to town next summer, for a full season as your mother would have done. He will always have your interest at heart, but that doesn't mean you must silence every feeling of your *own* heart."

Georgiana slowed a bit. "But I cannot trust my heart. It has already proven false."

Lizzy frowned. "That is what I was afraid of. There is a balance to be found between following every whim of your heart and... and distrusting yourself so." She seemed to recollect something. "Not that I mean to say you must act on every partiality. I hope you may live to find many men to your liking before you choose one!" she said gaily.

Georgiana shuddered. "Just the thought of all those balls and visits and breakfasts makes me feel sick."

Lizzy put an arm around her waist. "Never let Kitty or Lydia hear you say so! I am sure you will find it pleasant once you have begun. Your family seems to have ever so many connections; you will be welcomed everywhere. You will soon feel yourself among friends."

Georgiana shook her head. "Perhaps. But... Mr. Wickham seemed a friend."

"Not all men are like Mr. Wickham."

"No, of course not. But, do you not think there will be other men who are also tempted by... by my dowry, my inheritance?"

Lizzy frowned. "That may be, but… You will have your brother—and myself!—at hand to advise you this time. Between us we will send the fortune-hunters on their way."

"But you cannot *always* be with me," Georgiana said. "On the dance floor, at dinners, and so on. Oh, I dread it so! I will feel so tall and stupid, but everyone will pay me fulsome compliments because I am a Darcy…!"

{ 15 }

LIZZY TRIED TO COMFORT Georgiana. She assured her many times as they walked back to the house that it would not be the way she was picturing.

But... would it? Georgiana was a good-looking girl, tall like her brother, but not as pretty as he was handsome, which was most unfair. Lizzy had thought to reassure Georgiana that she would be welcomed and wanted everywhere, but that was not the problem. Georgiana had never been rejected anywhere, what she feared was a too-ready acceptance! Fortune-hunters and toadeaters and sycophants of that sort. What a different set of problems to have!

Lizzy rather thought she herself would not have been bothered by that. Were Lizzy to have a fortune, she would have flitted her way through society, rapidly judging whether her acquaintances were interested in her or her wealth and not giving the latter a second thought. She might not always have been correct, but that probably wouldn't have overly troubled her either. But Georgiana was not like her.

Georgiana would no doubt love to live somewhere where her wealth was not a factor, but there was no such place in the world. A small voice offered that the equality-promoting Methodists were perhaps the closest to that community to be found in England, but Lizzy shook her head.

She had offered Georgiana an opening to talk about Mr. Turner, and she had not taken it. This did not mean that Georgiana was indifferent to him—now that Lizzy reflected, Georgiana's letters had mentioned Mr. Turner far more than Lady Catherine's other guests—but surely if Georgiana felt deeply, she would say something. Eventually.

Lizzy had been excited about becoming Georgiana's sister, but that enthusiasm had been a bit short-sighted, hadn't it? If Georgiana had a mother, or other lady mentor, Lizzy would feel her own influence to be less. As it was… who else was in Georgiana's life besides her brother? Mrs. Annesley?

Lizzy was not easily overwhelmed, but she had certainly jumped into a more challenging situation than she had foreseen.

When Georgiana met the youngest Bennet, Miss Lydia, she rapidly lost her footing in the conversation.

"Why, you are taller than me!" Lydia said. "But not that much older. Why, you look just out of the schoolroom, which I daresay you are. I have been out for months and months, you know. Mrs. Forster, my particular friend, says I am more comfortable with her company than many an older young lady. That is why she asked me to accompany her to Brighton. We had such deliciously fun times! The officers quite longed to dine with us, I assure you, and more than once I had to warn them I was only fifteen!"

Georgiana did not begin to know how to reply to this. She looked to Mrs. Annesley, but that lady could not help Georgiana in the middle of a conversation. Her face looked particularly blank just now, which Georgiana interpreted as disapproval.

Lizzy grimaced. "Lydia, you ought not boast about such things. I am glad you are come home."

Lydia twinkled. "Yes, so am I, and don't you wish you knew why!"

"Because you are happy to be here for the wedding?" Lizzy said a little dryly.

"Oh, pooh, of course that, but I have another secret and you will not know a scrap about it until the wedding day!"

"Yes, well," Lizzy replied, "*if* you manage to keep the secret. You were never much of a hand at it."

"When I was twelve! I am sure I am much more mature now. Shall I be one of your attendants? I do hope so! I missed all the shopping, Kitty tells me, but you wouldn't leave me out for such a reason."

"None of us are leaving you out of anything." Lizzy softened. "I *am* glad you are back; I was a little afraid that you would be upset to have your holiday in Brighton curtailed."

Lydia waved her hand. "No, no. Even Brighton could grow flat. I don't at all begrudge the trip, I assure you. Besides, there is my secret!"

Georgiana smiled uncertainly. Perhaps it was some gift for her sisters? That would be a kind thing. Georgiana had rather looked forward to meeting the youngest Miss Bennet, the one closest to her in age, but they did not seem to have much in common.

Lydia flew through her house banging doors and greeting her family with loud exclamations. She swung her bonnet by the strings and twirled down the hall back to her and Lizzy.

Georgiana never banged doors if she could help it. She disliked loud noises. And she would not have enjoyed visiting Brighton and staying with an officer's wife, so it was difficult to enter into Lydia's raptures about her good times there. Georgiana could not keep saying, "How nice" without sounding like a dunce.

Jane entered the room, tying on her hat. "What time shall I return to Netherfield with you, Lizzy? Does Mr. Turner have a set time?"

"Oh! But are you going to Netherfield immediately? I just got back!" Lydia looked as though she might pout, but she switched like a flash. "Let me go with you! I have not seen Miss Bingley or Mr. Bingley in such an age. Or Mr. Darcy." She laughed.

Jane and Lizzy looked uncertain. "It is not exactly our place to invite you," Jane said slowly.

"No, but it is Miss Darcy's!" Lydia rounded on Georgiana unexpectedly. "Do invite me to come! It is so dull to come home and have everyone immediately leave me. You must understand, don't you, Miss Darcy?"

"I—Of course—If you should like to come—"

"Capital! I have the most ravishing new hat; I thought it too fine to wear merely for my trip home, but I shall put it on directly."

She disappeared, but Kitty took her place. "You are all going over to Netherfield? I never get to go! I am sure I like visiting as much as Lydia, and she has just been staying in Brighton while I have been stuck here at home. Why should she go and not me?"

Lizzy looked vexed. "I'm sure you have been there every week since I returned."

"Yes, but why should you and Lydia and Jane go and not me? Mary does not care for it, but I am older than Lydia and should get to go."

Georgiana opened her mouth, though she had not decided whether to invite Kitty or not, but Lizzy shook her head. "I think we shall be too many, too distracting for Mr. Turner. This is not a usual social call, you know."

"But—"

Lizzy threw Georgiana an apologetic look. "Then I shall stay here. You know, Kitty, it is more you that I rely on to help me on the wedding day. Jane shall be busy on her own account, and Lydia will never remember the things I need."

Kitty seemed to grow a little taller and straighter, brightening with the surprise and pride that Lizzy's words gave her.

{ 16 }

I T WAS THEREFORE A SMALLER party of Jane, Lydia, and Georgiana who returned with Mrs. Annesley to Netherfield. Georgiana apologized for showing them straight to the rear parlor. It seemed strange to do so, even though she knew that was the plan.

Caroline greeted them in the front hall, coldly nodding to Lydia and smiling rather forcedly at Jane. She escorted them up the stairs, but said, "My dear Miss Darcy, you needn't hide yourself away in the parlor all afternoon! You were already stuck there yesterday and this morning, were you not? Miss Lydia is here to keep our dear Jane company, so you are not needed. They will certainly excuse you."

"Well—"

"I swear we have not had a proper tête-à-tête since you arrived! I feel quite neglected."

"Perhaps another time," Georgiana replied quietly. "You must remember that neither Miss Bennet nor Miss Lydia have met Mr. Turner. I must introduce them."

Caroline was defeated but went away only after forcing Georgiana to promise she would find time for her soon.

Thankfully Mr. Turner was droll and comfortable, and Georgiana relaxed when he took charge of the party. He put Jane at her ease by first showing her the portrait he was doing of Lizzy, and then by mentioning that during the last two summers he had done portraits for both of his sisters before they married.

Lydia looked around, rather bored to be overlooked for Jane. She opened the door and peered out.

"I have never received a tour of Netherfield," Lydia said. "Do show me, Miss Darcy."

"I myself only arrived last week—"

"No matter! We can explore together. Do come. I daresay your woman can stay with Jane."

Mrs. Annesley looked more forbidding than ever at this casual reference to herself. Georgiana cast about for a reason to stay in the room, but she was no match for Lydia.

Lydia linked her arm with Georgiana's and before she knew it, they were traversing the second-floor hall.

"It is actually not so fine as I expected," Lydia commented. "I suppose since Netherfield is only *let* to Mr. Bingley they did not leave all their fine things. And I declare this rug to be nearly threadbare! I never suspected such a thing. Colonel Forster's rooms, though rented, were ever so fine."

"How—pleasant," Georgiana managed.

Lydia poked her head in each room, summarizing and expostulating and admiring in turn. She was not invariably rude, but even her compliments made Miss Darcy uncomfortable. This house did not belong to either of them. It was most improper!

Georgiana guided Lydia away from the family bedrooms and the study where Darcy was probably reading— surely Lydia wouldn't stick her head in there! Even though Georgiana prevented Lydia intruding on her brother, she couldn't help but hope he would hear the noise of the conversation and come to rescue her.

No such rescue occurred. They saw no one but servants. Possibly Bingley and Darcy had ridden out together, but Caroline must still be nearby. Georgiana nearly laughed aloud to realize that she was longing for Miss Bingley's company. Perhaps Georgiana ought to reconsider staying with the Bennets after the wedding.

When they had gone through the whole house, and Georgiana was as exhausted as if she had walked ten times that length, Lydia pulled her to the front door. "I have so much energy after my long trip home. Let's go walk in the garden. I declare I could run home if I wanted."

Georgiana pushed back a wild wish that Lydia *would* run home.

Instead, they walked in the formal gardens and Lydia kept up a running, and highly indecorous, monologue on her stay in Brighton.

Georgiana was still somehow unprepared when Lydia mentioned Wickham.

"Then there was Wickham," Lydia sighed happily. "He is a great friend of the Forsters, you see, and very much the gentleman. He danced with me twice that first night! And he would have taken me in to supper only that he felt pity for Miss Johnson and so took her in. He told me that she was a sweet girl—despite her sad resemblance to a sheep!—but that he would much rather have been my dinner partner."

Georgiana tried to murmur something intelligible, but her throat had gone completely dry.

"Oh, but you know Wickham, I was forgetting! I apologize if it distresses you."

Georgiana could hear her own pulse, the sound of blood rushing past her eardrums. "Did Mr. Wickham sp-speak of me?"

"Oh, well, we all knew that he'd fallen out with Mr. Darcy and lost the living that ought to have been his, but no one blames you. You must have been a child at the time."

Georgiana felt sick but endeavored to place one foot in front of the other in normal fashion. At least he had not told Lydia of their near-elopement.

"Actually, now I think of it, he said you were a very sweet girl and not at all like your brother. He said you used to be quite close." Lydia laughed. "Your face is so red! Did you have a *tendre* for him? I would not at all blame you!

He is such a handsome man. If he had grown up at Long-bourn, I am sure I would have been nutty on him."

This was too much. Georgiana cleared her throat, which was suddenly very thick. "I am merely warm and thirsty. I think we ought to go in for tea. Your sister must be nearly done by now."

She slipped her arm away from Lydia and led the way back inside. Her dismay and horror made her bold and she requested the butler to have tea served for them at once in the rear parlor.

John immediately perceived that Georgiana was upset. Her face was flushed, and she had a blind sort of look in her eyes. She didn't so much as glance at the canvas or Miss Bennet but instead looked out the window. She flinched when Miss Lydia came up to look out as well.

Georgiana requested Jane serve the tea, as Jane "would soon be the mistress of Netherfield, after all," and then re-tired to the seat farthest from the group. It was still not very far because the room was so small. He sensed Georgiana would have fled the room if she could do so and save face.

Mrs. Annesley also seemed to notice something amiss. She took the cup of tea for Miss Darcy from Jane and took it to her charge, placing a hand on her shoulder. She said something quietly and Miss Darcy shook her head once.

John drank his own tea, wondering what had happened. Miss Lydia seemed a good-humored girl, rather bold and careless, but not mean-spirited.

He was still wondering the answer when the time came for Miss Bennet and Miss Lydia to return home.

Georgiana and Mrs. Annesley saw them off, of course, and he remained in the parlor to work. Painting four *demi poires* before the wedding was rather a challenge, but the extra income was always useful. He had his own lodging in London to pay for—though if his private commissions continued at this rate, perhaps he would let that go and merely stay in a hotel when he was in town—as well as all the expenses of clothes, tips for servants, traveling charges, and so on. He also sent a modest amount to his parents every month.

Therefore, John remained in the room and worked most of the afternoon. He had sketched each lady on a separate sheet of paper, as well as marking them out faintly on the canvasses. With his sketches for reference, he could continue the painting without their presence. He might have them each sit once more for details of color and highlight, but he could do without if necessary.

John was still there when it was time to dress for dinner; he had to rush to get changed. He was more than a little disappointed when Miss Darcy did not appear for dinner at all.

"She has the headache," Mrs. Annesley told the group, particularly Mr. Darcy. "She was out walking with Miss Lydia for some time. Probably a touch of sun."

Dinner was tedious without Georgiana. In fact, everyone seemed in low spirits except Mr. Bingley. He hied off after dinner to visit the Bennets again, and Mr. Hurst fell asleep on a sofa with a book. Mr. Darcy bounced one booted heel up and down and finally rose. "Turner, care for a game of billiards?"

"Certainly." John was at least more proficient at billiards than whist, it being a popular game amongst the young men who'd been at the academy with him.

By the time they'd broken, and Mr. Darcy swiftly won the first game, they were on casual terms.

Mr. Darcy asked a few questions about his career and prospects, and John was emboldened to ask a little about Pemberley, his home. Darcy clearly loved the place and it was not hard to get him to talk about it.

"I gather Miss Elizabeth has not yet been there," John commented.

"No. I meant to try and do so in July, but I didn't want to leave Georgiana at Rosings for another few weeks. I made a quick trip myself, but it would have entailed a slower and longer trip had Elizabeth accompanied me."

Darcy missed his stroke. The cue ball glanced off the ball he'd attempted.

John circled the table and lined up his shot. "You could not have taken Miss Darcy with you to Pemberley?"

"I could, of course, but she had not been home in some time. It seemed inexpedient to take her on the lengthy trip and only let her stay for a few days."

John's ball struck true, striking the next ball with a satisfying crack.

Mr. Darcy sighed. "If I had grasped what was happening at Rosings, I would have done so regardless."

John raised his head. "I did not mean to pry—"

"No, it's fine. You seem a sensible, observant man. You were probably aware of the situation with Mr. Sutherland."

John wasn't quite sure how to look. He focused on his next play. "I was."

"I am not certain why I expected engagement and matrimony to be easier for Georgiana than myself. I've been the object of a few such schemes over the years, but I'm well able to shut such things down with a minimum of fuss."

John made his next shot, but not as well as he'd hoped, turning the game back to Mr. Darcy. "It is a pity that those least able to repel predatory persons and schemes are those most often targeted."

"True. Predatory persons…" he repeated, shaking his head.

John knew he ought not ask the next question, but he was not being wise tonight. "Is all well with Miss Darcy?" he asked. "One afternoon, when Lady Catherine bid her to bring down her portfolio, Miss Darcy happened upon a sketch of a gentleman which quite overset her."

Mr. Darcy's mouth tightened. He made his next shot, but rather too hard.

"I am not insinuating the least thing," John hurried to add, "only that I pitied her situation there at Rosings and I dislike seeing anyone unhappy."

"What happened to the sketch?"

"At her request, I put it in the fireplace."

Mr. Darcy slid his hand up and down the smooth wooden cue. "I suppose you realize I must ask you not to mention the drawing or her reaction to anyone else. For a lady of quality, any rumor... If it is necessary, I will make it worth your while."

John's mouth snapped shut and his jaw locked. "Absolutely not. I am not *extorting* you, sir."

Mr. Darcy's shoulders relaxed from rigid to merely straight. "I apologize. It would not be the first time." He moved to make his next shot. While not looking at John, he said, "She will be fine. She was merely the victim of a particularly vile fortune-hunter who had a score to settle with me."

John tried to school his expression not to show his own anger.

"Tell me more about these Methodist class-meetings of yours," Mr. Darcy said, changing the subject. "Is it true you can be kicked out of the church if you miss four in a row?"

John nodded, still trying to tamp down his feelings. "It depends. When you faithfully attend meetings, you receive a quarterly ticket with the date and so on. Without a ticket you are not considered an active member of the local church."

"That seems very harsh."

"We believe that accountability is vital to the soul," John explained, now taking his turn. "A man might have any number of godly intentions, but if there is no one who regularly inquires into the state of his soul, and of his behavior, he is soon lost. The heart is deceitful above all things; it cannot be trusted."

"So, these meetings are a sort of confessional, then?" Darcy asked.

"No. We pray daily to God for confession. Usually the meetings start with an elder or member who merely asks, 'How goes it with your soul?' We are committed to honesty and the regular meeting together. We reflect on our state and encourage one another in holiness."

John and Mr. Darcy continued to chat until Mr. Bingley arrived back, when John excused himself to his bedroom.

John hesitated outside of Miss Darcy's room for a moment. It was unthinkable to disturb her at such a time of day, in her bedchamber, but he still wondered what had upset her so badly that afternoon. He had only seen her that way when the drawing had surfaced, and his instinct told him today's trouble was related.

Sighing, John took himself off to bed. There were few ways to offer help or comfort to a lady who was not a sister, mother, or wife.

{ 17 }

GEORGIANA COULD NOT *SHUN* Miss Lydia merely because she'd mentioned Wickham. It was not at all that young lady's fault she found him handsome and believed his false stories. Georgiana had done the same!

But Georgiana also knew that she could not listen to such descriptions of Wickham, especially his words about *her*, with composure. She must endeavor to avoid much conversation with Miss Lydia.

To this end, she declined the next morning's visit to Longbourn in favor of the "long overdue" chat she owed Caroline.

Caroline smiled conspiratorially and when the gentlemen were gone, said, "I do not at all blame you for wishing to avoid the Bennet household! They are quite exhausting. I am sure there is not the least harm in them, but I never dreamed of having such connections."

This was too close to the truth for Georgiana to refute all of it. "I am ever so fond of Lizzy, and Jane as well."

"Oh yes, Jane is a dear, sweet girl. I have no objection to her for her own sake! But that family. I've told Charles more than once that they will take advantage of him."

"I don't think it." Georgiana cast about for another subject. "Will you and Mrs. Hurst remain after the wedding?"

Caroline sighed, rather dramatically. "I think I must go away, although I am so attached to Charles that the mere idea hurts. But I am very afraid that Jane, so sweet and compliant as she is, would leave the running of the household to me, and that would be very bad for her."

"Ah."

"No, we shall return to London; it will be a lovely change after the Hertfordshire assemblies and balls. You ought to come with me! I know you are not yet out, but Louisa and I should still adore your company! And you might go to a few quiet family parties, I think. Nothing more proper. Oh, do say you will."

"I am sure my brother would not permit it. I do thank you, but I think I shall be happier to remain here in Hertfordshire until I travel home with Bingley and Jane."

"But it would be such a pleasant diversion for you! It is high time you were introduced to the type of families you ought to know. You have such a small acquaintance, and it is only natural that you—that you shrink from…"

Georgiana frowned. "Shrink from what, pray?"

"That you shrink from associating with people worthy of you," Caroline explained. "I have noticed that you are so much more comfortable with people of... oh, a slightly lower order. I'm sure it is most natural! But as your devoted friend, I can't help but want you to value yourself as you ought."

"I truly don't know what you mean."

Caroline leaned forward and placed her hand over Georgiana's. "I first noticed it in small moments, your discomfort with the attention you received at the races, but your joy in the urchin who gave you flowers. Your discomfort with the true ladies you met in Tunbridge Wells and preference for Mrs. Annesley and Elizabeth. Even, from what you have said about your stay at Rosings, your discomfort with your aunt's guests and preference for plain Mrs. Collins!" Georgiana started to speak, but Caroline squeezed her hand again. "I don't at all wish to anger you, but I must add that since you have been *here,* I couldn't help but notice your preference for Mr. Turner."

Georgiana felt as if she'd been slapped. How indiscreet she must have been if Miss Bingley noted her preference for him!

"Do not worry, my dear Miss Darcy, I have only your interests at heart. I have a keen eye for these things," she added, quite truthfully, "and I only bring it up because I am so attached to you. You need an advisor near you, do you not? And your new sister-in-law is many excellent things, but I would not think advisor one of them."

Georgiana shifted uncomfortably, wishing desperately that she had just gone to Longbourn.

Caroline leaned back. "Do consider my offer to accompany us to London. I am sure Mr. Darcy would not begrudge you a few weeks of fun, rather than kicking your heels here, missing Mr. Turner. Better by far to distract yourself."

Georgiana looked instinctively to the open door. She would hate for him to overhear this.

"Please do not—"

Caroline interrupted sympathetically. "I recall my own first infatuation. The man was quite unsuitable—as first loves tend to be!—so you have my every sympathy. Soon you will look back and not believe you harbored affection for such a short, plain commoner. Why, Miss Darcy, you may look as high as any young lady in England."

She desperately wanted to defend Mr. Turner—he was not at all what Caroline said—but such defense would only confirm that lady's suspicions.

"I rather thought I might stay with the Bennets after the wedding," Georgiana said instead.

"With the Bennets? Both those crazy young girls? You will be miserable, Miss Darcy! Own that you would be miserable."

"I will not own anything of the sort. I am sure they would be a delightful distraction, if distraction I need."

Caroline could not be brought to acknowledge that it would be anything other than a penance, and Georgiana was too uncertain to argue for long. Soon they were discussing winter plans and Christmas. Georgiana was forced to exert some ingenuity to avoid inviting Caroline to Pemberley, despite Caroline's conversational traps.

And when they went down for a simple luncheon, where of course Mr. Turner was also having his midday meal, Georgiana could not quite meet his eye.

Caroline was snobbish and arrogant, but was she correct in this instance? Was Georgiana indulging a silly infatuation?

Georgiana knew, as Caroline didn't, that her *first* infatuation had been with Mr. Wickham. He had flattered and complimented and flirted with her. Mr. Turner had done nothing of the sort. He was not given to flattery and had certainly never flirted with her. Mr. Wickham had been handsome and well-dressed. Mr. Turner, though she had for some time now considered him extremely handsome, was always plainly dressed.

Surely her feelings for the two men were not the same.

But then, if she agreed within herself that this was not an infatuation, that it was nothing like the giddy bubble she'd felt for Wickham, did that mean she was in love?

{ 18 }

THE FEW FRIENDS AND FAMILY traveling to the wedding celebration would not come until the end of the week. As such, when Miss Anne de Bourgh, her companion, and Mr. Sutherland arrived late Monday, it was a surprise.

When the butler came up to announce their arrival, Caroline and Georgiana both were startled and displeased, but for different reasons.

Georgiana had not thought Lady Catherine would let Anne come, nor that Anne would want to! It wasn't customary for people to travel very far for weddings, so Lady Catherine could easily have denied the trip on that account. As for Mr. Sutherland, Georgiana hoped his visit was not to further his acquaintance with her.

Miss Bingley was similarly nonplussed.

Hertfordshire was not so far north of London that a day trip was impossible, so most guests would simply drive up Friday morning to be there for the wedding feast. Colonel

Fitzwilliam was coming to be Darcy's best man, and even he was not coming until Thursday evening. They had not expected any earlier guests.

"Don't worry, madam," Mr. Sutherland said after his introduction, rightly reading her reaction. "I am putting up in town at the Black Star. As a friend of Lady Catherine, and aware that Miss de Bourgh desired to be here for her cousin's wedding, I offered to escort her." He bowed. "It's been a pleasure, Miss de Bourgh. I hope that the journey has not been too taxing."

Caroline, having satisfied herself as to his gentility by the gloss of his black pumps and the cut of his coat, held out her hand. "Do stay for tea, Mr. Sutherland. It is the least we can do to repay you for your trouble."

"No trouble at all, but I shouldn't mind some tea. Miss Darcy, it is a pleasure to see you again so soon."

Georgiana curtseyed. She didn't *think* he would come all this way to further his suit—he had received no encouragement!—but then she did not understand men at the best of times.

Over tea he disclosed that they had also enjoyed the company of Mrs. Collins on their trip north. "We dropped her off with her family at Lucas Lodge—tidy little place!—and mighty glad they were to have her. They also offered tea, but Miss de Bourgh was growing weary, and I decided to come along without delay."

"Oh, I am so glad Charlotte could come," Georgiana exclaimed. "I know she very much wanted to attend."

Anne sipped her tea. "I think very highly of Mrs. Collins."

Georgiana blinked. Was this a mere pleasantry? From Anne it seemed praise indeed.

"A very comfortable woman, there is no doubt," Mr. Sutherland agreed.

Caroline was not much interested in this topic. She gracefully inaugurated a discussion of Mr. Sutherland's home and soon learned that he was the master of a large estate, one which rivaled Rosings. Her interest was piqued.

Georgiana, feeling quite cynical, hoped that Caroline would be successful in attracting that man's attention.

Mr. Darcy and Mr. Bingley arrived before long, and Mr. Sutherland took his leave. That might have had to do with the heavy stare Mr. Darcy sent his way.

Caroline went away to make sure the housekeeper had prepared rooms for Mrs. Jenkinson and Miss de Bourgh, and Georgiana moved closer to Anne.

"It was kind of you to come," Georgiana said quietly. "I know travel does not agree with you."

Anne sniffed. "I am actually rather better this summer. I believe the course of powders I began in Tunbridge has been beneficial."

"I am glad to hear that," Georgiana said honestly. "And that your mother permitted you to come."

Anne's nostrils flared. "She did not entirely like it, but Mr. Sutherland helped to convince her."

"I… I did not realize you had any desire to come."

Anne sipped her tea. "I did not. It is for Mrs. Collins's sake. She is my friend, and… friends help each other, do they not?"

Georgiana wasn't quite sure what to do with this blunt speech. "Yes, I suppose so. That was thoughtful of you."

Lizzy, meanwhile, was sequestered with her father in the library when their maid Sarah knocked and stuck her head in. "Mrs. Collins here to see you, ma'am."

"Mrs. Collins!" Lizzy sprang up.

She found Charlotte sitting in the parlor with Mrs. Bennet, looking quite stout and happy.

"Well, I have surprised you, Lizzy," she said.

"Surprised? I should say so! You said nothing of a trip home in your letters! I am so happy to see you here. Your family must be overjoyed. But how did you get here? When?"

Charlotte explained and Lizzy rejoiced in the circumstances, adding, "Mr. Sutherland? I am interested to meet him."

"But now Charlotte, tell us," Mrs. Bennet demanded, "you are increasing, are you not? There are only females present."

Charlotte was too well-acquainted with Mrs. Bennet to be surprised at this. "Yes, that's right. October."

"Well. I suppose your child will inherit Longbourn. I hope it does not trouble you to supplant Jane or Lizzy's children."

"It did, ma'am, but knowing Jane and Lizzy are so well-matched, I no longer regret it." Charlotte smiled at her. "Come, you have known me since I was born, and you know I am hopelessly plain-spoken. You are the envy of every mother in Meryton. You must not begrudge me my good fortune."

Mrs. Bennet fought a smile, but then recollected that she would rather be the smug but generous mother of two brilliantly married daughters than the victimized mistress of an entailed estate. "Well, it is true, Charlotte, and you were never one to mince words. They have done very well for themselves and no doubt. Even Lizzy…! Who I quite thought would never give Mr. Darcy another chance."

"I am glad she did, ma'am. In fact, I am quite eager to catch up with Lizzy. Do let us excuse ourselves and go for a walk. As a married woman and a mother, you know how precious it is to spend time with old friends."

"I do know; a mother sacrifices everything for her children."

Lizzy and Charlotte escaped outside, indulging in a comfortable gossip. They meandered toward oak on the edge of their property.

"Also, congratulations on the baby. I thought it might be the case when I was there in the spring, but I did not want to assume."

"Yes, you were right. But you did not used to stand on such ceremony with me."

"I—I apologize if I hurt you by not speaking. I *am* truly happy for you. You will be an excellent mother."

"Thank you." Charlotte put her left hand on the tree and with the other unconsciously rubbed her midsection. "Lizzy… for the sake of our long friendship, I would like to ask you a question. Would you consider becoming our child's godmother? If you… that is, if Mr. Darcy agreed?"

"Godmother?" Lizzy stooped and threw a pinecone into the pond. "Would not Lady Catherine object?"

Charlotte shook her head. "She would not like it right away, but only consider: Mr. Collins has no living relatives other than your father. His own father was an only child. So, you are his close relative and also my dearest friend." She cocked her head. "And not to put too fine a point on it, but in the event of tragedy, I would far rather my child went to you than to my next sister."

Lizzy *could* choose to decline. She could blame it on Mr. Darcy or the upheaval of being newly married—she had yet to even *see* Pemberley!—or some other excuse. Charlotte would take the rebuff with grace and their friendship would continue. It would continue *with* the distance that had developed since Charlotte's marriage.

Or she could accept. She could choose to move beyond tolerating Charlotte's marriage to supporting it. A godmother or father was often not deeply involved in the child's life. A nice gift on birthdays would be appreciated, perhaps Lizzy's presence at christening. If the child was a girl, Lizzy might someday offer to present her. If it was a boy, Mr. Darcy could perhaps help with a recommendation or living. More importantly, it was a show of affirmation for Charlotte.

There really was no question. "I would be delighted. Mr. Darcy has denied me nothing yet, I am sure he will be happy to acquiesce."

"Truly?" Charlotte asked, her voice breaking slightly.

Only now did Lizzy realize that Charlotte had seriously doubted Lizzy's answer. "Oh, Charlotte!" Lizzy gripped her friend's cold hands. "Of course. You have been my good friend for so many years. I hope that we will still be good friends when we are as old and autocratic as Lady Catherine."

Charlotte chuckled a little brokenly and wiped her tears. "Excuse my display; I have been more tearful of late." She resolutely recovered her composure. "Thank you, Lizzy. I know Jane is *your* closest friend; but you are still mine. Thank you."

Lizzy felt humbled. "I do care for you, Charlotte."

"I know. Now, tell me all about Mr. Darcy's proposal in Tunbridge Wells, so that I can say I knew all along."

{ 19 }

JOHN RUBBED HIS HANDS WITH A RAG soaked in paint thinner to get the thick smudge of oil off his thumb. He was not best pleased to hear that Mr. Sutherland was visiting. He had nothing against the man personally, but his suit had been rejected! It seemed bad taste to intrude on the Darcy family again so soon.

The skin on his hands grew red as he scrubbed at the spot. He ought to at least be honest with himself. He did not like the man because he had paid attention to Miss Darcy. He did not like him because he was the sort of man Miss Darcy would end up with.

Mr. Bingley and Mr. Darcy surprised him while he was still working on his hands.

"Still working, Turner?" Mr. Bingley asked.

"Just finishing for the afternoon."

John showed Mr. Bingley the painting of Miss Jane Bennet and was rather relieved at the gentleman's ready praise of it. No one could be so exacting as a besotted husband.

Mr. Darcy was harder to read. He studied the two portraits of Miss Elizabeth carefully. They were incomplete, but, if John was not overly humble, already captured that lady's charm.

"This one for Pemberley, I believe," Mr. Darcy said, indicating the one on the left. "You have actually come close to matching the expression in her eyes."

"Thank you, sir."

"When will you be done?" Mr. Bingley asked. "Darcy wants to give the extra to the Bennets at the wedding breakfast."

"They should all be done at least the day before. Do you wish me to procure frames, or would you rather do that yourselves?"

They both agreed that he would be a better judge of such things, and John made a mental note to allow time for a quick trip to London to buy what he had in mind.

"You should stay for the wedding breakfast," Bingley added. "I'm sure we'd be happy to have you; there's already going to be quite a crowd."

"A generous offer, but I don't want to intrude on a family affair," John said decidedly.

"Suit yourself," Bingley said, "But you're welcome to stay if you wish. In the meantime, care for a ride? You must get devilish stiff standing there all day."

"I am used to it."

"You may as well come," Mr. Darcy seconded this offer. "Bingley's horses need the exercise and then we will have another gentleman in case one of the ladies needs assistance."

From this John gathered that the whole party was going, and he was proved right when they assembled. That is, Miss de Bourgh was not present, she had chosen to lie down before dinner, but Georgiana and Bingley's sisters were attired to ride.

John did not exactly mean to position himself beside Georgiana again, but he certainly did not fight it.

She was quiet for a time, but then broke the silence. "Do you suppose people have to be taught how to be friends?"

"It certainly comes more naturally to some than others."

"Yes. It must be partly one's innate qualities, but also how they are taught... and how it is modeled."

"Undoubtedly. Then there is the spiritual aspect," John said. "Kindness, selflessness, humility, love; all of those are gifts of the Spirit and must be cultivated. I do not believe they are not the natural state of humankind."

"Do you not think so?" asked Georgiana. "I am not talking of wicked people. Only ordinary people like you or myself."

"The Scripture says that we are all wicked but for regeneration. Even our best actions are not pleasing to God if they are done for ourselves."

"Then how do you believe we cultivate kindness and selflessness and so on?"

John stuck his hand in the inner pocket of his coat and pulled out his quarterly ticket. "On the edges are the ordinances of my church."

Georgiana held the reins with her right hand and took the ticket in her left. It was neatly printed, but the date had been written in by hand and the ink was a trifle smudged. It was dated in March of that year, and titled, "Quarterly Ticket, Methodist Episcopal Church." A verse was just below. "God is love, and he that dwelleth in love, dwelleth in God, and God in him. 1 John iv, 16."

The paper had a small flourished border, and on each edge of the rectangle were commands.

"Read the Scriptures – Regularly Contribute." She turned the paper. "The Supper of the Lord. Family and Private Prayer. Punctually attend Class and Public Worship."

Georgiana studied it. "I pray, of course, and there is a Bible in the library at home that I sometimes read. When I was younger, I wanted to know more, but of late years I haven't thought of it as much."

"That is partly what our community does; it prevents the discouragement and numbness of life from silencing that voice in our soul."

"That's…a beautiful thought."

John forced himself to look away from her. "We memorize Scriptures to that end. Psalm 19 is one of my favorites. 'The heavens declare the glory of God; and the expanse shows his handywork. Day unto day pours forth speech, and night unto night reveals knowledge. There is no speech nor language, where their voice is not heard.'"

He fell silent.

Georgiana studied the verse on the ticket. "I have memorized so much music, so many poems, but not many passages of Scripture. I shall have to rectify that."

Darcy dropped back to join them.

"Trying to convert my sister?" His smile was edged.

"If I can," Mr. Turner said, somewhat surprising himself.

Georgiana also looked startled. She handed back the ticket. "Thank you for showing me. I do like that you—that your church encourages dialogue on serious spiritual matters. My school was very progressive, but they didn't equip me to deal with the complexities of life, guilt, or—or purpose…"

Mr. Darcy's eyebrows drew together. "But you are not burdened by guilt, Georgiana, or by those 'complexities of life.' You can trust that I will take care of you."

"Oh, I do. But guilt is something— I mean, everyone must feel—"

Mr. Darcy shook his head. "Too much dark talk on a beautiful day. Come, Georgiana, let's ride ahead to Longbourn. We will stop there for a few minutes before we return."

When Mr. Darcy arrived with the riding party, Lizzy allowed him to extract her, leaving the Misses Bingley,

Hurst, and Darcy with her family. She knew Jane would stay nearby this time, lest Miss Darcy get overlooked. Lizzy often walked out with Mr. Darcy when he visited; she knew he preferred the outdoors to a prolonged coze with her mother and sisters, or even her father.

Mr. Darcy looked troubled. "I probably ought not to have come just before dinner, but…"

"You have trailed off," Lizzy said eventually. "Which is most unlike you. I would obviously attribute it to love of me, but I suspect that was not what you were about to say."

He smiled at her, as he invariably did when she teased him, but he still looked disquieted. "I am a little anxious. I fear Georgiana might be growing overly pious. I thought she was recovering from Ramsgate quite well, but perhaps I was wrong."

"Overly pious?" She chuckled, but then her earlier intuition came to mind and she bit her lip. "Has she been speaking with Mr. Turner?"

"Yes. Though I daresay she might have come upon the idea even without his influence. It hadn't previously occurred to me, but for a sensitive girl like her, feeling guilty and shamed over the incident with Wickham, this is a very possible reaction."

"Is piety so terrible?"

"No, but hearing her talk just now… I fear she is a few steps from a nunnery."

"I think she is more likely to become a Methodist."

Darcy cocked his head quizzically. "Because that is the particular brand of zealotry she is exposed to just now?"

"I think…" Lizzy struggled with how much to say. "I think because she cares for Mr. Turner."

Darcy stopped walking. "Excuse me?"

Lizzy winced. "I am not at all sure, only it has once or twice seemed to me that she is not indifferent to him."

"Mr. Turner? No, I do not think you can be right. John Turner for Georgiana Darcy? It is ridiculous."

Lizzy faced him. "As ridiculous as Elizabeth Bennet for Mr. Fitzwilliam Darcy?"

"No. No, that is not what I meant."

"Isn't it?"

A faint color rose in his cheeks. "I admit you have reason to think so, but truly the circumstances are different. My attitude toward you and your family was quite wrong, I have owned it. But your father is a gentleman, you are clearly a lady—it was my pride that was at fault. Mr. Turner is essentially a tradesman, from a large working-class family—it is quite different. It is not what our mother would want for her."

"Perhaps your mother would have liked Mr. Turner."

Darcy smiled. "Touché, she very well might have. My father, on the other hand…"

"Would they have approved of me?" Lizzy put her hand on his arm as his eyes grew distant. "I don't want to wound you, but I think you might consider that times *do* change. And you are the one here."

"It is easier to make decisions for myself. For Georgiana… Lizzy, I wish my mother was still alive."

Lizzy turned pink.

"Wishes are nonsense, of course." He visibly drew himself together, the rare vulnerability disappearing. "Shall we return to the house?"

Lizzy put one finger to his lips to stop him. "You called me Lizzy."

"Oh? Yes, I suppose I did—"

Lizzy stretched up on her toes to kiss him, the first time she had initiated such a thing.

Darcy was surprised, but quickly caught up to her mood. Without thinking, his hands came up to grip her waist. Lizzy pulled away and laughed, kissing him once more before continuing to walk.

Darcy reached for her hand. "If I'd realized calling you Lizzy would get such a reaction, I would have begun weeks ago."

She laughed again, blushing slightly. "It is not only that. It is… oh, that you would discuss Georgiana with me; she is so important to you! And that you called me Lizzy without thinking. You are generally so formal."

"I have not intended to be formal with you."

"I know; but your personality is reserved and your manners strict. I told someone, soon after I first met you, that I would need to start by being impertinent or else I should soon grow afraid of you."

"Not *afraid* of me, surely."

"Not now. But I realize I have fallen out of the habit of getting past your reserve and I must not. And if you will occasionally call me Lizzy and tell me what is behind that handsome, stoic face of yours, we will go on swimmingly."

Darcy felt himself blush like an idiot.

Lizzy laughed.

"I have felt the…distance, but I do not know how…"

"It is like a hedge," Lizzy said helpfully. "A hedge of formality that grows between us. We must regularly trim it, and all will be well."

They were distracted for a few minutes, but eventually they came back to the topic of Georgiana.

Lizzy swung their joined hands. "I don't know if there's anything more than a slight partiality on her part. Perfectly common in girls her age. Only I can't help but think that if it *is* a lasting attachment… it might be the very thing for her."

"The very thing? Setting aside matters of status, they have nothing in common in birth, education, or interest."

"You yourself were just pointing out that she appears drawn to the fervency of his belief! But beyond that, you have forgotten personality. Even from the little I have seen, I would guess them to be well-suited, both earnest, serious souls, with a shared love of art and music. Can you not picture Georgiana learning all the Methodist hymns on the pianoforte? I imagine she would find far more satisfaction in playing for a community like that than in displaying her skill in the refined drawing rooms of London."

"She would have to, for the drawing rooms would be closed to her. She would be forsaking the society to which she was born."

"Are you not being a trifle dramatic? I think it more likely that she would raise Mr. Turner to her level. He is already gentleman*like*, and with an unquestionably genteel wife, such advancement would not be unheard of. Even if he was not accepted as such, her family would never cut the connection. I do not think Georgiana would mourn the rest of high society."

Mr. Darcy sighed. "She probably would not, but hopefully this is an unnecessary conversation. In all likelihood, even if she enjoys his company, he does not think of her."

Lizzy maintained silence.

Mr. Darcy's brows rose. "Oh?"

"I do not think he is indifferent." She thought rather more than that but did not think Darcy could take it yet.

He looked comically dumbfounded. Lizzy kissed him once more for good measure. "If it is that unnerving to you, we probably ought to return to the house and not leave them alone."

{ 20 }

GEORGIANA COULD NOT COMPLETELY avoid Miss Lydia, but she assumed the buffer of seven other women and two gentlemen would be sufficient to avoid difficult conversation. She even welcomed Caroline's clinging presence by her side; although Caroline *had* asked what Mr. Turner said that was so interesting on the ride over. Georgiana was glad that she could recount only a religious conversation and wipe the smug look off Caroline's face.

She almost thought the visit would end successfully, but she reckoned without Lydia.

Before they left, Lydia came and sat beside her. "I have only been home for a day, and I am already sick to death of wedding talk. If it were for my own wedding, that would be different, but it is so dull to be forever speaking of someone else's preferences! And I try to tell Jane and Lizzy they are being ridiculously parsimonious with the arrangements—as if your brother could not afford all the best!—

but they will only talk of fitness and decorum and such stuff as that. Tell me, is it true you have a dowry of *£30,000*?"

Georgiana blanched. Caroline gave a disdainful cough. Thankfully, Lydia spoke quietly. But who would Lydia have learned that from if not Mr. Wickham? Oh, it was too much.

"It cannot be… suitable to discuss such things," Georgiana muttered.

"Oh, pooh. Don't be stuffy, I pray you! If *I* had £30,000, I should be ever so happy about it. I should not be so mean and stingy as some people," she eyed Lizzy darkly, "or so quick to preach economy to those with less! I daresay you have never even worn a hand-me-down dress or a refurbished bonnet."

Georgiana felt both embarrassed and ashamed. Of course, Georgiana did not have four older sisters, and she could hardly wear her brother's cast-off clothing, so it was a silly question. But she did recognize the difference in Lydia's lot versus her own.

Caroline smiled derisively at Lydia. "Why should she? Or are you angling for her to pass on her bonnets to you? I daresay Miss Darcy would not mind; she is always charitable."

Georgiana threw out a hand, somehow hoping to stop the conflict that threatened. Before she could come up with an answer, Mr. Turner took a few steps toward them. "How do you do, Miss Lydia? Your elder sisters tell me you have been in Brighton. Did you enjoy the sea-bathing?"

Georgiana could tell this was his way of saving her, of adroitly changing the subject, and her cheeks burned that he'd heard enough of the other conversation to know she needed saving! Also, it was not an entirely happy change of topic. Brighton led quickly to balls, which led to officers, which led to Wickham.

He was clearly one of Lydia's favorites and his name often popped up in the silly and improper anecdotes she recounted. Georgiana's remaining strength was sapped by the repeated mentions of him. She felt she was only a breath away from fainting or being sick or begging Lydia to stop.

Caroline looked even more haughty and snide. "I know Wickham was long a favorite of your family. Was not he quite Miss Elizabeth's favored swain last fall?"

Georgiana already knew, through Elizabeth, that Wickham had quite deceived her, but hearing it was still a blow. Georgiana simply must become accustomed to hearing his name. She had to be calm. No one except her brother, and now Lizzy, knew she was in any way connected to him.

But then Lydia laughed. "And Miss Darcy knows him better than me! They have known each other forever, and did you not meet again in Ramsgate last year? Is Wickham not a handsome man? A modest, agreeable, talkative man?"

Georgiana breathed shallowly. "On the contrary, I am no longer friends or even acquaintances with Mr. Wickham. He has been such a… trial to my brother."

Mr. Turner's clear blue eyes fixed on her with understanding. Georgiana pulled her gloves through her fingers nervously.

Lydia scoffed. "Oh! If you will believe only what your brother says...! I have it from Wickham himself that he has tried several times to reconcile. And made those overtures in spite of the financial difficulties he finds himself in due to Mr. Darcy's cruelty. I—"

"Excuse me." Georgiana began to rise and put back on her gloves. "I cannot listen to such criticism, such falsehoods about my family. I can only say that my brother has been... faultless in their falling-out."

Lydia curled her lip. "As you like."

When they were mounted again, Caroline lost no time in condemning Lydia's behavior. "She has no sense of tact or propriety. I quite blushed to hear her. You should have given her a much heavier set-down."

"I don't think she means any harm," Georgiana said weakly.

"I don't think she *means* anything, that would imply she had more than two thoughts in her head!"

Georgiana shook her head, unwilling to be drawn into such disparagement.

The ride home seemed to be full of avoidances. She did not want to criticize the Bennets. She did not want to talk with Mr. Turner in front of Caroline. She did not want to interact with Mr. Sutherland at all. Her brother was in conversation with Mr. Turner, and she did not want to interrupt them.

This was becoming an awkward house party, indeed.

Georgiana was often anxious about the feelings and opinions of those around her, but this was worse than normal.

As she rode home, for the first time, she began to resent the difficulty she was in. Was there another way to live?

She did not wish to be like Lydia, but... the way disapproval slid off the young girl's shoulders was astounding. Georgiana would never be callous or indifferent to those around her, but what if she simply did what she wanted and let them think what they might? What if she enjoyed talking to Mr. Turner and let Caroline think what she would? What if she conversed with Mr. Sutherland like a normal person and took no responsibility for his misplaced hope? What if she told her brother that she was quite serious about not coming out next season? Georgiana shivered at the idea of conflict with her beloved brother. But what if she did? It still seemed impossible to let go of her fears, but at least she could see the horizon of such determination. She had approached the edge and peered over.

In an act of defiance invisible to the naked eye, but very real to her, Georgiana urged her horse forward to ride abreast of her brother and Mr. Turner.

{ 21 }

ANNE DE BOURGH ENTERED THE bright and sparkling Netherfield dining room on Mr. Bingley's arm, as was appropriate for the highest-ranking lady present. She'd never had the smallest particle of interest in Mr. Bingley. He was handsome, winning, and his hair seemed to shine as bright as the candles. He was too much. What had such a person to do with her: plain, ill Anne de Bourgh? Miss Bingley was also fashionable and beautiful and, as they would have said in a pagan society, kissed by the gods. Anne spied nothing in her but insincere flattery and smug pity.

However, while in the past Anne would probably have relapsed into a vaguely disgusted silence at dinner, Anne was preoccupied by another problem. A knottier one.

She had wanted to do Mrs. Collins a favor, and the idea of enabling her to attend this double wedding had fit the bill perfectly. Unused to forming and executing her own plans, Anne was rather exhilarated that it had worked.

However, she was no fool, and she knew that her mother would have flatly vetoed it but for the continued perseverance of Mr. Sutherland.

Therefore, Mr. Sutherland had done her a favor and she needed to decide whether he ought to be repaid in kind. She did not think of him as a friend precisely, but he had acted as one, and so perhaps he was owed the reciprocity of friendship.

She had only recently been inducted into the fellowship of adult friendship, something that had seemed opaque and uninteresting until now.

So, whether to try and do a kindness for Mr. Sutherland was her next decision, and if so, what. On their journey from Rosings, she learned much about his estates and a little about his son and first wife. He was not a passionate man, but he had been quite attached to his wife, and losing her had clearly been an unexpected and devastating blow.

She could not ameliorate his family state in any meaningful way, but perhaps he had mentioned something, though slight, that she could affect.

As it happened, she was just as silent at dinner as usual, but she was much more pleasantly occupied. She ignored the strange byplay that seemed to be passing between Mr. Darcy and Mr. Turner, as well as Georgiana's short responses to Miss Bingley. People thought Anne did not notice things, but she did. She usually did not care.

She found to her interest, however, that thinking of what she might do for Mr. Sutherland engendered kinder feelings toward the man himself.

She had noticed the same thing before, namely that she felt more friendly toward Elizabeth Bennet after doing her a favor. Also, her real affection for Mrs. Collins had increased with the effort of securing the wedding trip.

Anne wondered if anyone else had stumbled upon the efficacy of good deeds to promote good feelings. Perhaps one reason she had not felt much affection in her life was due to her inability to do people good. She had been too ill to do much good for the people of Hunsford. She had been too retiring and unexceptional to bring her mother much joy. She had been too sullen and unhappy to bring her governess much pleasure. Even Mrs. Jenkinson, who had been with her for years, had been terribly excited to have a "break" from her presence.

Ever since Mrs. Jenkinson returned, Anne could not see her in the same light. The older woman was paid to act like a friend, and that distinction was newly recognized. Anne still accepted the care and fussing of Mrs. Jenkinson, but she knew there was little to no affection behind it. Anne had the uncomfortable thought that she had never given the woman much reason to like her.

The ladies retired to the drawing room while the men had their port, and Anne was still lost in thought.

Georgiana, just to her right, conversed with Caroline. Georgiana tried once or twice to include Anne in the conversation, but Anne replied shortly. Georgiana was another of those people who knew nothing of difficulty or suffering. Anne felt as if they barely spoke the same language.

Caroline did not seem to care about Anne's reticence and continued to pester Georgiana about visiting her in London.

Anne was still pondering the surprisingly thorny problem of doing Mr. Sutherland a service when Miss Bingley went to consult with a servant and Georgiana interrupted her thoughts. "You seem most serious tonight, cousin. What occupies your mind?"

Anne sighed. It did not occur to her that Georgiana's eagerness to talk was more a symptom of her own problems than a desire to bother Anne. Nonetheless, Anne was accustomed to telling the truth, so she explained. "I am considering how to do a favor for someone."

No one was attending to them, and Georgiana lowered her voice. "May I ask who you wish to benefit? If it is Miss Bingley, I could recommend—"

"No, why would I do her a service? It is Mr. Sutherland."

"Oh."

"The things a lady can do, the favors she can give, are quite limited, are they not?" Anne found herself explaining. "I know, for instance, that he likes horses, but what good is that? He already maintains quite a stable for himself and his mother, and even if I wished to give him a hunter, he would probably not accept."

Georgiana had a thought. A daring though. A defiant, probably stupid thought. "Do you like Mr. Sutherland?"

"I know no ill of him. He was helpful in escorting us to Hertfordshire."

This was not much encouragement, but Georgiana had heard worse from Anne. "You could… you could offer to marry him."

Anne somehow narrowed her eyes while also raising her brows. She looked very like Lady Catherine. "You jest?"

"No…no. I know it is much more than a favor, but I know that he misses his wife and desires to remarry. He is approved by Lady Catherine. He lives near to your home, so you would not be going quite out of your neighborhood. It would be a most eligible match as far as family, fortune, and society. It would protect the heritage of Rosings, as that will someday be yours." Georgiana paused. She was talking too fast, too eagerly. Part of her motivation was to get rid of Mr. Sutherland as a suitor, the other part was to do Anne good. Georgiana was not a critical person, but even she recognized that her aunt was a cold, controlling woman. If Anne was healthy enough to leave, she might have a much happier life.

Anne was frowning. "I never truly thought of marriage."

"Truly? Even with my br—" Georgiana broke off.

Anne ignored those words. "I am better presently, but I might have a relapse at any time. I do not know if he would want an ill wife."

Georgiana was shocked that Anne's first thought was that she was not good enough for Mr. Sutherland, rather than vice versa. Georgiana was learning far more about Anne this summer than all their previous visits combined!

"You could ask him if that bothers him," Georgiana said boldly. "I think he would be honest." Her conscience smote her, and she added, "But you must ask yourself if you could come to love him. It would not be fair to yourself or him to marry otherwise."

Anne wrinkled her nose. "You have such romantic, plebeian ideas."

"Well...if you could feel respect and affection, then," Georgiana amended, knowing many people agreed that love was unnecessary for marriage.

Anne nodded slowly. "It is an idea. It is certainly an idea."

When the gentlemen joined them, Georgiana was again requested to play. As fate would have it, Mr. Sutherland joined Anne on the settee.

Georgiana played a short, lively song. It was not considered rude to talk quietly after the first piece, so she purposely got it out of the way quickly. Then she began a slower, quieter melody. She strained her ears, wondering if her venture into matchmaking might possibly bear fruit.

Probably not. Even self-possessed Anne de Bourgh could not abruptly propose to a gentleman…

But no! Anne was turning to Mr. Sutherland.

"You convinced my mother to yield and allow this trip," she began. "Would you consider us friends?"

Georgiana used the left pedal on the piano, the una corda or soft pedal, to mute her music slightly more. She had never wanted to eavesdrop so badly.

Mr. Sutherland's broad face broke into a surprised smile. "Why yes, if you would consider me a friend, I would be happy to count myself so."

Anne nodded. "Then, as a friend, I would like to do you a favor."

"You needn't repay me for this trip, I was happy to come on my own account."

"Be that as it may, I was wondering if..." Anne looked up at her and Georgiana continued the song, looking away. She'd let her fingers linger too long in one position, her gaze drifting irresistibly to the event happening only feet away from her.

"I know it is somewhat irregular," Anne said slowly. (Was the unflappable Anne de Bourgh *nervous*?) "But I wish to ask whether you are interested in having a wife. In remarrying, I should say. I daresay you haven't thought of me, and I might not be at all what you would like, but you may consider me as an option."

Georgiana didn't dare look at them again. She felt her ears might fall off if she listened harder.

"Why, Miss de Bourgh, this is very brave of you. I like that you are not afraid to mention it. Why there is so much fuss about the process of these things, I do not know. Women are bound to be as interested in the outcome as men, so why should they not discuss it?"

"Yes," Anne said. "Would you like to discuss it? You are aware that I am the heiress of Rosings, and I already know of your estates in Surrey and Kent."

"It would be a logical union, most appropriate," he agreed. "I am a widower, but you know that. My son has a nurse; you would not be saddled with his care, but you would be around him."

Anne nodded. "I do not have much experience of children, but I should be willing to try. My health would probably not allow me to...do as much as many ladies would, however. I have been somewhat better this summer, but I cannot promise it will last."

He spoke gravely, "For your sake, I hope that it shall. But I have found to my grief that even a robust constitution guarantees nothing. I should be willing to hope for the best, and if not, I have some experience in caring for a sick wife."

The end of the song came upon Georgiana unexpectedly. Scattered applause greeted her, but she only wanted them to be quiet!

Sadly, by the time Caroline had taken her place at the pianoforte, Anne and Mr. Sutherland had stopped speaking. Georgiana was left to wonder, but the strange expression on Anne's face, something like disbelief mixed with pleasure, gave Georgiana hope.

{ 22 }

JOHN WAS BUSY AT WORK THE next morning before the family and guests were down for breakfast. He had still several steps to complete and needed to use his time well. He'd set up his second easel so that he might work on one portrait and then leave it to dry for half an hour before moving it while he worked on the next.

Currently, he had both portraits of Miss Elizabeth Bennet on the easels. John wondered if someday they would create machines that could do something like this; reproductions of a single image multiple times. He could not imagine a machine getting tone and nuance of color right—how would it blend the paint or wield the brush?—but then no one thought yarn and cloth could be woven by machine, but the textile world was entirely different than it had been fifty years ago.

John selfishly hoped mechanization was not on the horizon for portraiture. But if it was...well, Lord willing, he would adapt. Perhaps he would go to America after all and begin a new career there.

He had begun to feel that anywhere within a hundred miles of Georgiana might be too close. He had, however, every intention of walking away at the end of the week without saying any of the things in his heart. How much he cared about her, how happy they would be, how much more he wanted for her mind and soul than her society encouraged.

Surely once he wasn't seeing her every day, it would be easier. Once he was back in London and she was up in Derbyshire, he would not see her unless he undertook a trip to do so, and he would never present himself at Pemberley uninvited. No, he just had to get through the end of the week.

It had strengthened his resolve to learn she had a dowry of thirty thousand pounds. Several thousand would have been helpful. Even as much as ten thousand would have been a blessing on their lives. But thirty? It rose like the cliffs of Dover between them, a dividing line no less impassable for being invisible.

He had almost convinced himself on their latest ride that he might have hope, and then he had overheard *that*. Miss Darcy had not confirmed it, but she hadn't denied it either. He rather thought she would have if it wasn't true.

Why, if her fortune was invested in funds, as it probably was, the interest would easily be a thousand pounds a year. Roughly his current annual salary.

John jumped a little when the door opened. It was Mr. Darcy.

"You're up early," John said.

Darcy shrugged. "I am accustomed to country hours. And I could not sleep with the oppressive atmosphere."

John nodded; the humid, hot morning probably indicated a coming storm.

Mr. Darcy had been acting a little strange last night, directing several searching stares at him and asking some odd, unconnected questions. John waited, but Mr. Darcy did not seem inclined to elaborate.

John went on painting.

"You mentioned once that you are from a large family. Where was your home?" Darcy asked.

John explained and answered several more questions about his family.

Mr. Darcy left almost as abruptly as he'd come. John could only wonder. Did Mr. Darcy suspect that John was in love with his sister? If he did, wouldn't he rather throw John out of the house or give him a stern warning, not inquire about his family?

It was strange.

Mr. Darcy didn't know himself what he hoped to gain from speaking with Mr. Turner. He supposed he was doing it to prove to Elizabeth that he would not reject the man out of hand. He wanted to say that he had given Mr. Turner a chance.

Honestly, before Lizzy enlightened him, he already liked Mr. Turner. He had done so since the blessed man sat in silence with him that first evening at Netherfield. Since then, Darcy had found him educated, conversable, and interesting. He was solid and sensible. With a better acquaintance, Darcy could easily imagine coming to highly respect him, and Darcy did not respect people easily.

But that did not make Mr. Turner any more acceptable for Georgiana's hand. Did it?

He entered the dining room where a light breakfast was set out on the sideboard. Miss Bingley was already serving herself tea, rather earlier than her norm. Perhaps the weather woke her as well.

"You look morose this morning, Mr. Darcy. Is anything amiss?"

"No." He had hardly finished a breakfast of tea, beef, and boiled eggs before Mr. Sutherland came calling. He was staying in a hotel in town and did not usually appear at Netherfield first thing in the morning.

"Have you eaten, sir?" Miss Bingley offered. "You're welcome to breakfast."

"You are all kindness. I apologize for intruding so early. I only need a moment of Mr. Darcy's time."

Darcy was nonplussed. If the man had come here to offer for Georgiana again, when nothing had changed since the last time, he was an idiot. But Darcy was trying harder not to assume people were idiots without sufficient proof, so he acquiesced dubiously.

He was nearly as surprised by the man's question as the first time.

"You wish to marry Anne?"

"Yes. I know you are not Miss de Bourgh's guardian, but you are the head of the family, and I know it would weigh with Lady Catherine if I have your support."

"Not right now it wouldn't," Darcy said bluntly. "You'd do better not to mention me."

"That is a point. Ticklish matter. Particularly since Miss de Bourgh was expected to wed you."

"That was never our arrangement," Darcy snapped.

Mr. Sutherland waved a hand apologetically. "No, so I apprehended. No offense meant. Truly. It just seems so much simpler to me to discuss the way things are! I hate those conversations where we must guess at meaning from elliptical words and looks."

Mr. Darcy relented a little. "If you wish to be blunt, I have no objection. Anne has been rather better the last few months, but she might always be invalidish. Also, she is very attached to Rosings. I suspect she would not look favorably upon your offer."

"No, on that you may be easy; she herself suggested it."

"Ah… Surprising." Darcy took a moment to adjust his thoughts. "In that case, I suggest you apply to Lady Catherine at once. As she approved you for Georgiana, she can hardly deny you for Anne."

"That is plain-speaking, and I am glad to hear that your thoughts tally with mine. I don't hesitate to say that the

Rosings estate would be a fine thing to add to my own; both in size and location it is ideal."

"For Anne herself..." Darcy hesitated, trying to think how Elizabeth would encourage him to speak. "I have never been close to her, but I have sometimes thought she did not benefit from her isolation."

"Sure enough and I agree with you there. I'll be honest that furthering my acquaintance with your sister was part of my plan in coming, but I found Miss de Bourgh, after we were twenty miles out from Rosings, unbent quite remarkably. She and that friend of hers were quite happy, and they both, though neither of them beauties, improved immensely with cheerfulness. That's the thing with women, isn't it? A little kindness and indulgence can work wonders. And having their own way doesn't hurt!" He chortled at his own play on words.

Mr. Darcy shook Mr. Sutherland's hand. "I hope you can make her happy, then. Despite her illness, I don't think she has experienced much kindness or indulgence, not indulgence of the right sort anyway."

"Trust me for that. Besides, I saw at a glance that your sister is still gone on that painter fellow. That won't last, but girls will take these fancies. At least she chose to get hung up on a God-fearing Methodist and not some dandy or rake."

He didn't wait for an answer before exiting the study, whistling a cheerful tune, blissfully unaware his final words were not as comforting as he thought them.

{ 23 }

LIZZY WAS DELIGHTED THAT HER Aunt and Uncle Gardiner were arriving that morning. They had taken rooms in Meryton, claiming they didn't want to "burden" Mrs. Bennet in the midst of supervising the baking of the wedding cake. They also "didn't want the children to tax Jane and Lizzy," who were usually their chief entertainment.

Lizzy suspected that Mr. Gardiner merely knew his limits and that his sister in high alt was beyond them.

Lizzy had taken some pains to ensure that she could introduce them to Mr. Darcy without her family nearby. If he could only meet her uncle with no knowledge of who he was, that would be even better! She was certain that the good understanding and intelligence of each would recommend them to the other. Unfortunately, anonymity was out of the question. Elizabeth had not given up on privacy.

Mr. Darcy, by prearranged plan, picked her up in Mr. Bingley's open phaeton at Longbourn and drove her to town.

"You are late." Lizzy was surprised but not accusing. "That's unusual."

"I apologize. I had an unexpected visitor."

"Ah." She twisted her hands in her lap.

"You are nervous," Mr. Darcy accused. "Do you not trust that I have learnt to mend my manners?"

"I do trust it. But it is not manners only that I want... Oh, I want you to love them as much as I do! But I know that is not a fair burden to put on you. Let me only say that while we no longer speak of my family's impropriety, I am not insensible of it. If Jane and I have anything of better feeling and manners, it is my aunt's influence."

"Lizzy, look at me."

She raised her eyes to his. "I love you. I am happy to meet the family you love."

As it turned out, the meeting was everything Lizzy could have hoped for. Her aunt had grown up in Lambton, the town nearest Pemberley, and fond reminiscences of the people, places, and particulars began them on a happy note. Her aunt displayed her normal intelligence and humility; there was neither height nor false deprecation in her re-membrances. Yes, she had met his parents on several pub-lic occasions, but mainly knew of them by report. No, she did not know the person he spoke of, unless he meant her dear friend Gertrude's son...? He did.

They soon recalled themselves and apologized for embarking on a discussion that Lizzy and Mr. Gardiner could not participate in. Mr. Darcy then politely asked about their summer excursion, adding that it was kind of them to shorten it for the sake of attending the wedding feast.

Her uncle waved that away and gave a brief overview of their trip, with some judicious praise of northern England. A chance remark led them to discover that they both enjoyed fishing, though rarely had time for it. It was a short step from there to Mr. Darcy telling him that he must come to Pemberley someday and fish the lake with him. "It is well-stocked but under-fished."

After canvassing a few more topics ranging from the rioting in London—reforms in the House of Commons—to their shared love of Lizzy—"the niece we have always doted on!"—it was time for him to go. They would take Lizzy home later, but Mr. Darcy had a few purchases to make in town.

After he left, Lizzy sighed. "You like him, don't you?"

Mrs. Gardiner looked up curiously. "Surely there was no danger of that!"

Mr. Gardiner shook his head. "Quite the gentleman. But don't worry, my dear. I would not claim a visit on the invitation Mr. Darcy offered in passing. But it was very affable and friendly of him to offer."

"Indeed, he has not any unbecoming height in his manners," her aunt agreed. "I cannot account for your previous descriptions of him."

Lizzy blushed. "Nor can I. I was blinded by prejudice."

"But we had heard such things...has he at all accounted for that business with Mr. Wickham? Or perhaps you have not tried to discuss that with him."

"On the contrary, I threw it at him quite forcefully when he first proposed." Lizzy went on to explain some of what had happened, not naming Miss Darcy but making clear how thoroughly Wickham had fooled her.

"Not just you, but all of us!" Mrs. Gardiner was dismayed. "There was such a look of openness and honesty in his face... But now that I have met Mr. Darcy and heard the truth of this, I do see the impropriety of Wickham's actions. What a bold liar he is, for I can characterize it as nothing less."

"I am glad Lydia is home," Lizzy added, "for it sounds as if they were becoming quite friendly. He never paid her much attention here, but I was somewhat afraid that my connection with Mr. Darcy might make him take note of her."

Georgiana felt restless with Darcy gone, and when she felt restless, she played the piano. Her mind kept straying back to her cousin Anne, wondering if anything had been decided.

This pianoforte, in Miss Bingley's style, was noticeably fashionable. The wooden panels were decorated in the Chinese style, with strange shapes and patterns. The edges of the panels were lined with black, glossy wooden trim. The tone was... well enough. Nothing to scoff at, but still not to compare with the sound of her piano at Pemberley. That one was of plain blonde wood, well-crafted and perfectly toned, but nothing extraordinary to look at.

She played several scales and arpeggios, mindful that she had not truly *practiced* in many days. Eventually however, she let her hands go to her favorite pieces.

Mrs. Annesley slipped in with some white work in her hands and settled down across the room near the window. Her niece was having a baby and she always made and embroidered a special garment for every new member of her family.

Georgiana didn't immediately notice when another figure paused outside the door. Not until he shifted, then she saw Mr. Turner leaning against the door frame, listening.

She smiled a little and somehow, when one song led to another, found herself naturally playing her favorite pieces, even the romantic sonata she had played for Wickham.

As the notes fell like raindrops from the instrument, Georgiana felt that two paths were opening up before her. There was Mrs. Annesley, who represented everything peaceful and proper in her life: a woman Georgiana genuinely loved. Then there was Mr. Turner. He represented something else, something exciting, challenging, and profound.

Mrs. Annesley could not see him from where she sat, nor could Mr. Turner see her companion. Georgiana was balanced between the two. He did not enter the room but continued to lean against the threshold with his eyes shut, enjoying the music.

Georgiana loved him in that moment, but she knew she could not choose him. Her future, like every young lady, was not her own to give away. But her heart was hers, and she could acknowledge what she felt for Mr. Turner. For John. Because she *was* in love with him.

She loved his square face and smudged hands and broad shoulders. She loved his intense beliefs, his self-control, and his gentleness. She loved his art and skill and humility. She loved him.

She would not fancy herself a tragic character—many women loved when there was no hope of marriage, or like Anne, chose to marry without love—but she was quietly glad to acknowledge it was real. It was far more real than the guilty infatuation Wickham had encouraged in her. Perhaps someday she would feel something like this for another man, and she would know it was worth pursuing.

She finished the song and he opened his eyes. Could he read her mind? He looked at her seriously for a long moment, then bowed. "Thank you, Miss Darcy."

He strode away, back to his paintings probably, but Mrs. Annesley looked up at the sound of his voice. "Who is that, dear?"

"No one. He's gone."

{ 24 }

GEORGIANA COULD HARDLY CONTAIN a squeal of excitement when Anne took her aside after lunch and shared the understanding that now lay between her and Mr. Sutherland.

"I know you will keep this news quiet," Anne said with a quelling look, "as he has not yet spoken with my mother."

"Of course." Georgiana wrung her own hands to resist hugging Anne. "Are you happy about it?"

"I am," she said calmly. "My mother told me that Mr. Sutherland was a sensible, well-bred man, and she was very right. I find him easy to talk to and...and *worth* talking to."

"And his son?"

Anne tilted her head. "I do not have much experience of children, but I do not mind them. We shall see. Like you, I lost my father at a young age. I do not know the pain of losing a mother, but I can sympathize with it." She paused. "I had forgotten that you and I had that in common. I have never told you, Georgiana, but I am sorry that you lost both your parents so young."

Georgiana tried not to gape. "Th-Thank you. It was difficult."

Anne's gaze trailed upward introspectively. "I think I have been, perhaps, too ready to think only of my own difficulties. It has sometimes blinded me to those of other people."

Georgiana did hug her this time. "You seem to be making up for that now."

"Yes. Well." Anne returned the hug a little awkwardly.

Had Lady Catherine ever been physically affectionate? Georgiana couldn't help wondering what that would mean for Anne's marriage, but she supposed that would be Mr. Sutherland's problem to overcome.

And it was none of Georgiana's business. She blushed at her own thoughts; when had she gotten so...carnal?

Anne smoothed her skirt. "I think I will lie down; I have the headache a little." She turned back to add primly, "Thank you for the suggestion."

Georgiana was too happy and excited to sit sedately with Miss Bingley and read or write or embroider. She was too jumpy to play the piano any longer.

What a wonderful thing for her cousin! And Georgiana had...had done it! She was too humble to think it all her doing; most likely Mr. Sutherland would eventually have turned his eyes on Anne and Rosings. But still...that might have taken a long time!

"Mrs. Annesley." She knocked on that lady's door. "I am desperate for a walk. Would you care to accompany me? I shall not go beyond the edges of Netherfield."

Mrs. Annesley also had the headache and charged Miss Darcy not to stray too far from the house and to come back the moment she felt a drop.

Making this promise, Georgiana retrieved her bonnet and escaped outdoors. The clouds were low and gray, but a fitful wind had picked up that relieved the hot stillness of the morning. It fanned her cheeks and gave something of wildness to the sedate garden around Netherfield.

Georgiana was startled to turn a corner of the garden rows and come upon Mr. Turner. She had assumed, when he didn't appear for lunch, that he was still working. He was seated on a stool in the corner of a path, quite hidden from the house by a large pot of flowering hyacinth.

He had a small canvas and easel before him and was occupied in painting the scene of yellowing autumn fields, brown avenues, green hedgerows, and the gray clouds above it all, promising an autumn storm.

"Miss Darcy," he said at once, standing.

"Mr. Turner." Her self-revelation of the morning almost caused her to turn away immediately, down the path that curved away toward the house. But, flushed from her victory with Anne, Georgiana stayed. Her new knowledge warmed her from within. Why should she not spend a few minutes with a person she enjoyed? It was not improper for a lady and gentleman to be together out of doors, in broad daylight, in view of the front windows of the house.

"You are doing a landscape, I see. That must be satisfying." Georgiana moved to see it better, and he sat back down.

"The four portraits are all but done. Otherwise I would not waste my time like this."

"I do not think you know what wasted time is," Georgiana said. "Most people who painted this in an hour would consider it time well-spent indeed."

He smiled a little. "Thank you. At any rate, tomorrow I plan to take the portraits to London to get them framed. Then I shall be back on Thursday to return them to Mr. Darcy and Mr. Bingley."

"You should stay for the wedding breakfast then, since you will hardly leave again that night." Georgiana flushed a little at her forwardness. "If you wish, that is. Lizzy says they have soaked the fruitcake in such spirits that it will last forever, and their cook has been preparing good things for weeks."

He only smiled, his face in profile as he flicked his eyes between the painting and the foreground. "That sounds delightful. I don't know that I like the way these fields look. The Dutch do such wonderful things with twilight and half-light. If I ever wish to move that direction, I must practice." He paused. "You are so proficient with the pianoforte; you must know the necessity of practice."

"Yes. At first it was only a requirement, but the last few years it has been quite a solace. When I am practicing something challenging, I cannot think about anything else."

"Yes, exactly."

His canvas wobbled in the wind, and they both reached out to steady it. John's fingers rested over hers for a few seconds before Georgiana slid her hand away.

John looked up at her. Unspoken words hovered in each of their mouths, but Georgiana, though learning to be bold, was not going to start something she knew would end sadly.

John still felt the warmth and softness of her fingers under his. He nearly threw caution to the wind. But what kind of man would he be if self-control was overthrown by the merest touch? He had come out here to clear his head after watching her play the piano. He had come to drown out the feeling that his very heart was touched. Exactly how far could he flee temptation?

He and Miss Darcy stayed, her hand clutched to her chest, his bracing the painting.

That is, until a roll of thunder caused her to look up. Then her eyes darted towards the painting and she exclaimed, "Oh, no! The rain will ruin it."

As if coming out of a trance, John shook himself. His bare head was becoming damp, and raindrops were beginning to pelt his shoulders and arms. "Oh. I must— the paint—"

His mind was still a little dazed and he struggled to think what to grab and how. He cared more about his specially made wooden case that housed the vials, powders, and ingredients for his oil paints than the new painting itself. But he ought not leave the borrowed stool here to get soaked...

Miss Darcy knelt and clicked his case shut, lifting it. "I can lift this and the palette. You bring the stool and the rest."

John obeyed and they made an awkward run to the house. He carried the easel and painting together, gripping it tightly and smearing the edge of his clouds. The stool banged against his shin, but he did not feel it.

They stumbled into the foyer of the house, and the Netherfield footmen, who were not ordered to keep a sharp eye on the door like they would in London, did not appear immediately.

John set down the stool and put the painting on top of it. He closed the folding easel and leaned it against the wall. "I certainly feel foolish! I knew it might rain but planned to come in sooner. Thank you." He took the palette from her. "Oh, I think you have got some paint on your dress."

Miss Darcy squinted at the side of her skirt. "I will ask my maid to wash it out before it dries."

"It might not come out at all," he said apologetically. "The pigment will, but the linseed oil is tenacious. That's why I usually wear a smock."

He took the case of paint from Miss Darcy and again their hands touched. Rather unavoidable on the short handle.

Her hair was not drenched, but the strands that had blown free curled damply around her face. Her shoulders were also quite wet. "You—ought to get dry," John said stupidly.

Georgiana shivered, as if to confirm his statement. "Of course."

"Miss Darcy," John said as she left, "I'll be sorry to leave Netherfield after the wedding. This has been... a wonderful summer."

She hesitated in the door but only half turned her face. "For me as well."

{ 25 }

T HAT EVENING CAROLINE WAS MORE importunate than usual, urging Miss Darcy to stay with her after the wedding, and even repeatedly calling upon Mr. Darcy to agree.

Georgiana was endeavoring not to be depressed at the absence of John—Mr. Turner, that is—who'd retired immediately after dinner. She forcibly directed her attention to more cheerful subjects. Mr. Sutherland and Anne were the chief of these.

But Caroline drew near Georgiana again, while she sat at the piano looking idly through the music, and put her hand on Georgiana's shoulder. "Georgiana, you must prepare for your season, and how better than to attend a few quiet soirées with myself and Mrs. Hurst? We can invite a few intimate friends, so that you will not be quite surrounded by strangers next spring. Indeed, you can be in the pleasant position of introducing Miss Elizabeth to *your* friends when she brings you to town."

Darcy murmured something noncommittal, and as he was entirely indifferent to both Miss Bingley and the next season, it cost him nothing. Georgiana was uncomfortable.

A little later Georgiana spoke softly to Darcy. "Could I speak to you for a moment alone?"

He looked up at once. "Of course."

In the library, he faced her and clasped his hands behind his back. Georgiana felt rather as if she ought to recite the catechism. The last light of twilight glowed in the windows to the west, casting a faint pink glow on the room.

"I— I do not wish to go to town with Miss Bingley." She started with the easiest part.

He blew out a long sigh. "I thought not. You know you may remain here at Netherfield with Mrs. Annesley. Or, as you suggested, we could ask the Bennets to host you. It is not my favorite idea, but if you wish it..."

Georgiana shook her head. "I no longer wish that either. I love Lizzy very much, but Mary and Kitty and Lydia...we do not have much in common. They will visit me, which will be pleasant, but I will stay here." Georgiana licked her lips. "But that is not the main thing I wished to tell you."

Darcy furrowed his brow.

She took a deep breath. "I know that I need to stop considering myself a child; you have said as much. I need to learn to exert myself in company and behave as one of my position ought to do. You have also said that I do not need to consider marriage at once."

Darcy nodded. "Several solid premises. Why do I fear the inference will be less to my liking?"

"I do not wish to be presented next season."

Darcy exhaled wearily. "This, again? Our mother—"

Georgiana raised a hand. "Please..."

He inclined his head to let her continue.

"I only knew our dear mother when I was a child; I never knew her as an adult, never saw her as her own person. Your knowledge of her will *always* trump my own. But I do know myself." Georgiana swallowed. "I do not wish to be presented yet. I know it is not something I can escape forever; I can even admit that someday it might be something I desire, but right now it is the opposite. And this request is not merely due to the shyness you accuse me of. I was not particularly shy of Mr. Sutherland, even though I was aware he was hoping to court me."

Darcy frowned at the mention of Mr. Sutherland, but Georgiana hurried on. "I only mention him to explain that I am not *afraid* of my season. But we both know that my dowry is larger than that of the usual young lady. That information will make my first season more fraught than it might be for another girl."

"I will protect you from fortune-hunters and the like," Darcy protested. "I will send them to the right about."

"No doubt you will, when they ask for my hand." Georgiana let the rest hang in silence. He would not be with her at every visit, every dinner, every ride or dance...

Darcy rubbed a toe on the carpet. "I know it will still be difficult, even with my protection." Heaven knows he had hated the matchmaking schemes directed at himself. Why would he think they would be less bothersome to Georgiana? Like Turner had said, predatory persons always seemed to find those least able to repel them.

Darcy frowned harder as he thought of that man. "Does this have anything to do with Mr. Turner?"

A look of pain crossed her features. Darcy winced.

"No," she answered. "Except in that...he has made me aware that there are other options for my life than the one society expects of me."

Darcy was not in the habit of speaking of such things with his sister. He wanted to ask whether she loved the man, but even as his mouth framed the words, they would not come out.

The silence lengthened between them. Darcy truly was torn. If she had made peace with forgetting Mr. Turner, or indeed, had never cared for him so deeply, he was loath to upset that.

Finally, he said, "Your request to postpone your coming-out is reasonable. Let us say that it ought to be done by the time you are twenty. Unless you should already be married by that time."

Her brows rose a little on that caveat, and her mouth quirked, but she nodded. "Thank you." Her voice wavered, "Indeed, thank you, Fitzwilliam. I thought you would be much harder to persuade."

A True Likeness

He embraced her. "I am sorry if I have been dictatorial on some points. I cannot let go of everything, but I will try to remember that you are a lady with your own mind now. And if I should forget, I am sure Elizabeth will remind me."

{ 26 }

FRIDAY, THE DAY OF THE WEDDING, dawned bright and beautiful and chilly. Lizzy was awake before the rest of her family. She slipped on her plain shoes and ran out to the large oak tree to see the sunrise. The storm earlier that week, which had apparently heralded the end of summer, had turned the roads to sludge, but thankfully they were beginning to dry out. There were two graceful gray and white herons ankle-deep in the pond. The still surface of the water reflected the gnarled boughs of the oak and the glowing peach of the sky.

Lizzy had always thought it most unlikely she would be married, but here she was on her wedding day. It was a momentous thing to cease being a Bennet and become a Darcy. It was a good thing. But it was also strange.

She heard footsteps approach and turned to see her father coming up to her.

He smiled sadly. "My last morning with you."

"It is not the last." Lizzy leaned against him, side to side. "Unless I die on the journey home, we will both live to visit the other and have many more mornings together!"

"Do you already think of Pemberley as your home? I suppose that is good, but this selfish old man doesn't like it. You were always my little Lizzy."

"I am—" Elizabeth broke off. She could not assure him that she was still his little Lizzy. She had grown up; she'd made mistakes, decisions, and compromises. She had been humbled and humiliated, but also honored with trust and friendship she did not expect or deserve.

"I suppose I *will* be Elizabeth Darcy," she murmured. "But I will still be Lizzy on clear summer mornings with my dear father."

She saw that his eyes were filled with tears and that started her own. "Oh, Papa."

She clung to him, letting her tears fall, hoping it would comfort him to know how much she would miss him.

Eventually she used her handkerchief to blow her nose and wipe her cold, wet cheeks. "I must not be red and swollen on my wedding day. And you must remember that you still have three daughters at home."

"The other girls are not like you."

"No, perhaps not. But they could be better companions than you think." He took her arm and they ambled back toward the house. "You might train Kitty and Lydia to think on more things than men; I know it must be possible. And Mary very much wants to be wise and well-read like you. If you were to let her sit in your study now and again, and talk with her, I think she would very soon give up martyrs for philosophy. Then you would have someone to talk to."

He sighed ruefully. "That sounds very wise in theory and very difficult in reality. And we both know I deal better in theory."

This was only too true, and as they entered the house, her father retreated to the library. "Please tell your mother I'll be ready at ten."

For once, Lizzy's mother and sisters were up betimes. Lydia was in particularly excellent spirits. She sang as she dressed, a saucy song of love and courtship.

"Gracious, Lydia," Mrs. Bennet said. "Wherever did you hear that?"

"In Brighton, of course!" She laughed. "Oh, it's almost as if it were my own wedding day."

"You'll have your chance, Lydia dear," Mrs. Bennet said placidly. "With your sisters so well-situated, who knows what kind of grand match you might make!"

"I don't need a grand match as much as a grand man!"

Mrs. Bennet pushed her toward the stairs and the dining room. "Do you get along. But wait!" She looked into Lydia's room, "What is this pile? Have you laid out every dress you own? Was something amiss?"

"No... I could not decide what to wear. Sarah can put it away later!"

"Normally yes, but all the servants have extra work today."

Lydia only laughed. "Then she may do it tomorrow! I do not care."

Georgiana drew her finger down the cold windowpane in her room. The wedding day. She dressed for the event in one of her favorite dresses, a pale green satin with a sheer white overskirt. Her dark green pelisse matched it perfectly, and she would want the pelisse if the morning was as cold as it looked.

The servants at Netherfield were busy arranging for the wedding feast, which Mr. Bingley had offered to host at Netherfield. Mrs. Bennet had ordered some of the refreshments from the merchants of Meryton, and it seemed every ten minutes another gig arrived and drove around to the kitchen entrance. She'd been told there would be "several prime hams, a few rounds of Mr. Henley's best cheese, and a crate of lemons to make lemonade for the ladies." Mrs. Nicholls, the housekeeper, could be heard marshalling the staff in a raised voice.

Georgiana lingered over her toilette until Mrs. Annesley scratched at her door to ask if she was ready to go down.

"You look lovely," Mrs. Annesley said. "A happy day for us all."

"Yes." Georgiana said. Except that today she would also say goodbye to Mr. Turner. Her philosophy of love and loss was not quite as sanguine as it had been a few days ago; she was finding the idea painful.

"It is a happy day," she repeated. She was *overjoyed* for her brother, and she would not allow her own small heart-break to ruin the day.

Georgiana and the rest met for a very light breakfast before the ceremony. There would be such a feast afterward, at eleven, that Miss Bingley had requested just tea, muffins, and sliced turkey for this meal.

Though it was morning, Mr. Bingley and Mr. Darcy were dressed in their evening finery for the wedding. Very dashing. The ceremony itself would be only the closest family and the witnesses to sign the register. The two couples could have just been witnesses for each other, but Darcy had chosen to ask Colonel Fitzwilliam to be his best man and witness. Lizzy had told Georgiana only yesterday that Charlotte would be her witness.

Other than those few, it would only be Georgiana, Lizzy and Jane's immediate family, and Bingley's sisters. The rest of their friends and family would join them outside the church and ride in several carriages to Netherfield.

John brought the finished and framed portraits down during breakfast. Bingley was delighted with Jane's portrait. "Capital! I shall have it hung directly we return from Portsmouth."

Georgiana and her brother were less demonstrative, but she hoped John knew how pleased they were. Mr. Darcy also smiled upon Georgiana's portrait. "Elizabeth told me how she badgered you into it. I am glad. I ought to have had done so anytime these last ten years."

He desired a servant to take up the two for Pemberley to pack, and the extra of Miss Elizabeth to be put aside in the large room where the wedding feast would take place.

Mr. Bingley sat back down. "Glad you decided to stay, Mr. Turner."

He looked at Georgiana. "Me too."

{ 27 }

GEORGIANA HAD NEVER BEEN TO a wedding ceremony and was quite enthralled by the details. She'd read the ceremony in her Book of Common Prayer quite recently—wondering how the Methodist wedding would differ, if she must be honest—and it was just as solemn as it sounded.

The vicar read the vows for Mr. Bingley and Jane first. Jane looked more ethereally beautiful than ever in her pale pink gown with flowers in her hair. Her voice was soft, but firm. Georgiana wanted to listen carefully, but Lydia, who sat nearby, kept fidgeting. She moved back and forth on the bench, smoothed her curls under her hat, and moved something that crinkled in her reticule. Her expression, when she turned her head, looked downright mischievous.

Georgiana had never done such a thing before—it was a week of firsts—but she finally leaned forward and shushed the other girl. Lydia's eyes snapped up to her, looking rather angry, but then dissolving into a silent smirk.

Georgiana looked away. The register was pulled out. Jane and Bingley signed, followed by Lizzy and Darcy as witnesses. The marriage lines were taken out and given to Jane, as was customary.

Then it was Lizzy and Darcy's turn. Jane had spoken the words like an angel, but Lizzy spoke them with more energy. Her eyes twinkled with joy and sometimes mirth at the antiquated wording of the vows. When Darcy recited the last portion of his vows, Georgiana wiped a stray tear. "With this ring I thee wed, with my body I thee worship, and with all my worldly goods I thee endow: In the Name of the Father, and of the Son, and of the Holy Ghost. Amen."

After that, the vicar said several prayers, read several portions of the Scripture relating to marriage, and finished by administering holy communion to the couples.

Lydia did not make it silently throughout the whole, but she did subside whenever she noticed Georgiana's eye upon her.

Perhaps it was a lingering annoyance that caused Georgiana to be more aware of Lydia for the rest of the morning. When they exited the church, it seemed the whole town had turned out to cheer and throw rice and seeds. The marriage of two daughters from a prominent family to two men of fortune was apparently quite a draw.

The carriages were parked at the end of the lane leading to the church, allowing for a bit of a procession. Georgiana and the rest of the family walked just behind the two couples. Lydia smiled, waved, and called out to her friends, but she looked rather downcast as they reached the carriages.

"Are you feeling quite the thing?" Georgiana asked her.

"Yes, I am fine. This was such good fun! I should dearly like all this fuss made over me someday, but for people who… But no matter. What did you mean by shushing me as if you were my aunt or grandmother? You are such a strange girl."

At Netherfield, the ballroom had been set out with many chairs and small tables for the wedding breakfast. The large dining room table had been removed there as well, to hold the food and the all-important wedding cakes, which graced the center of the table. Georgiana had heard several footmen swearing with words she'd never heard as they struggled to move the table last night.

By the time everyone had arrived, greeted the newly married couples, and actually begun to eat, Georgiana felt the feast ought to have been called the wedding *lunch.*

Mrs. Bennet and Jane and Bingley received many compliments on the arrangements.

"Oh yes, it is unusual," Mrs. Bennet answered one woman, "But with two daughters and such a beautiful space to use…! And I simply knew we must have two cakes for two brides. Mr. Bennet begrudges nothing for his girls."

The cakes were browned from the oven and thick with fruit. Georgiana's piece was delicious, and she knew that many people would go home with one more piece to save for later. Wedding cake was easy to preserve.

Fewer people spoke to her or to her brother, but Georgiana was thankful for it.

John, who leaned with his back to the wall, watching the festivities, noticed that Georgiana was somewhat alone. This was not her town, of course, but he couldn't help thinking that she didn't belong in a deeper way. She had yet to find a community that fit her.

He wondered what she would make of his family.

"Have you had the cake?" Georgiana asked. "It's wonderful."

He shook his head slightly. "No, but I am quite full, thank you."

"Oh, I forgot about the alcohol in the cake. I'm sorry."

"Nothing to apologize for."

They stood there silently. John wished to talk to her one more time, but what was there to say? There would be a thousand things to talk about if she were… his. But as it was, he was leaving.

He was not sure if she felt as deeply for him as he did for her, but she felt something. If he was allowed to court her, he was sure he could win more. But with the decision made, there was very little to say. He could not speak of weighty things, and he did not have the spirit to speak of light things.

"Where is Miss Lydia?" she asked unexpectedly.

"The youngest Bennet girl? I thought I saw her…"

They both looked, but Georgiana shook her head. "She isn't here."

"Perhaps she stepped out to the powder room, or…"

Georgiana bit her lip. "Possibly. I cannot explain, but I have the feeling there is something wrong. Please excuse me." She left the room and returned some ten minutes later. "Unless she has gone to the kitchens or is hiding in a bedroom, she is not in the house."

"If she grew tired, perhaps she lay down?"

"At one in the afternoon? With cake to eat?" Georgiana bit her lip. "I think I must ask Mrs. Bennet."

But that lady looked around vaguely when asked. "Lydia? No, where is she got to? I am sure she just stepped out."

"I didn't see her in any of the rooms downstairs."

"Why, what a strange… Do enjoy the party, my dear! Your brother doesn't get married every day! Don't worry your head about anything. Now, Mrs. Lucas, I see that you will be a grandmother soon! What a joy to you. Of course, he will not live so close to you as dear Jane's children will be to me, but then, we can't have everything."

Georgiana wasn't sure whether to persist. She did not like to make a fuss about nothing. Perhaps Lydia *had* chosen to lie down or… or something. Perhaps Lydia was indulging her curiosity about the rest of the house? But Lydia did not seem like the type to miss a party, and Georgiana had heard several of the Lucas girls excitedly questioning her about Brighton. Why would Lydia walk away from such encouragement?

"You are still concerned," John said. "Did Lydia say something to you?"

"No… no." Georgiana wracked her brain. "She did say something about a surprise for her sisters on their wedding day. I suppose it could be that."

"You think a gift? Perhaps she got her groom or coachman to drive her home to fetch it."

"Yes, but why not bring it with her? Or send it on ahead if it was bulky?"

"If it is a surprise…"

"*If* it is. It is not quite rational, but I feel so uneasy about her."

Caroline broke away from a conversation with an artificial laugh and smile for Mrs. Long, and tucked her hand in Miss Darcy's arm.

"What is amiss?" She led Miss Darcy a few steps away, speaking even softer, "You have spent far too long whispering with Mr. Turner in the corner. You must guard your reputation, my dear Miss Darcy."

Georgiana moved impatiently. "I noticed some time ago that Miss Lydia is missing from the celebration. We were discussing where she might be. If she might need… assistance."

"Even if she does, she does not need it from you. I daresay she felt ill from the copious amount of lemonade and cake she consumed and went home to digest. You must cease thinking that these people have a claim on you."

"That is possible." Georgiana's fears, rather than diminishing, were becoming more concrete. "I can't help but wonder if she had some plan of her own for today."

Was it only because of Georgiana's own near-elopement with Wickham that the thought of such behavior occurred to her? Did she have any reason to suspect Lydia of such a scheme?

Unfortunately, she rather thought she did. Lydia had a "secret" for her sisters. She was full of such nervous energy she could not sit still during a wedding. Was that a letter she had tucked into her reticule? And now she had disappeared. Worse, she had spoken of Wickham specifically and repeatedly; she had resented Georgiana's defense of Darcy. Was that Wickham's influence?

"Excuse me, Caroline," Georgiana said. "I think I must make sure that she is well. Would you send orders for your coachman to drive me to Longbourn? I will return directly."

"Alone?"

"I suppose I will take Mrs. Annesley. I don't want to bother the others. It is probably nothing."

Caroline, who had an uncanny scent for scandal, was intrigued. "If you are uneasy, I will accompany you. If there should be something untoward, we hardly want the servants involved."

Georgiana bristled at this description of Mrs. Annesley, but Caroline had a point. "Let us go quickly, then."

John was still nearby, and Georgiana paused, telling him the small plan. "I am sorry to leave so abruptly. I hope to be back before you go—"

"May I offer my escort to you both?" John said. "Otherwise I will be wondering the outcome of this small mystery all the way back to London."

Caroline curled her lip, but John ignored her. "My curricle is already harnessed; I planned to depart soon. We can be there and back in a trice."

{ 28 }

GEORGIANA FELT RATHER SILLY when the Bennets' second housemaid responded to their prolonged knocking. The girl looked quite blank. "Oh! Miss! Sir! Excuse us not hearing you right off. The servants is having a bit of a jolly on account of Miss Lizzy and Jane getting married."

"Has Miss Lydia been home in the last hour or so?" Georgiana asked.

"Why, yes. She asked Tom to help her load the band-boxes in the wagon, the bandboxes as held the presents she bought for her sisters in Brighton. Though where she got the pin money to buy ever so many gifts, I am sure I don't know! Tom said they were right heavy."

"But the Bennet carriage—"

"Not that one, ma'am. She got Ted, that is young Mr. Lucas, to drive her from Netherfield in his gig."

"Oh..."

Caroline cut her off. "Of course. But the thing is, she forgot something. We will just go up to her room and find the last gift."

On the stairs, she whispered to Georgiana, "Even if something truly untoward has occurred, you must take care what you say to the servants. It is not fitting that they be involved in family affairs."

"I know, but…"

Lydia's room was a mess. Mismatched walking boots and slippers dotted the floor. Every surface was littered with discarded dresses, ribbons, hats, and stockings. The number of hats seemed to indicate that she had emptied several bandboxes for this expedition.

One corner of her writing desk was clear, and on it there was a letter addressed, "To Mama."

Georgiana frowned for a moment, but Caroline grabbed and unfolded it. "Heaven forefend, has she actually run away?"

Georgiana took the note in shivering hands and read.

Dear Mama,

Kitty has been a good sport in keeping my delicious secret, but now I am laughing because it is done! Wickham sent me notice yesterday that he waits for me in Hatfield, and from there we shall catch a stagecoach.

Do not be angry, Mama! I did not want to keep it a secret from you. I so wanted to tell you that you were marrying off three daughters today instead of two! How happy you would have been! I knew you would sympathize with us, but Wickham straightly forbid me to tell anyone.

He was afraid that odious Mr. Darcy had poisoned the whole family against him. And he was not wrong! I found out at once that Lizzy completely turned against him. Wickham told me it would be so from the outset. He warned me, the first time our emotions overcame us, that he must never think of reaching as high as my family now that Lizzy was to marry Mr. Darcy. I had to assure him that I was not in danger of such disgusting snobbery. Can you imagine? I am not so fickle!

So today I will go to meet him as he has planned. He says even if someone should follow us, he will not give me up. Oh, Mama, I never thought I should have such a romance! And with such a wonderful, handsome man!

I was singing that song just now, the one I learned in Brighton, and neither you nor Jane nor Lizzy thought anything of it! Oh, how I laughed. "To Gretna Green shall we go, if Papa's answer is no. We'll ride through the night in a cross-country flight, like an arrow shot from a bow…"

But I know Papa's answer would be yes, only Mr. Darcy is so proud and rich we must not cross him! But now I have made it all right. Mr. Darcy cannot blame you if you did not know!

Wickham is right, it is so deliciously appropriate for this to be our wedding day as well as theirs. Well, perhaps not our wedding day. I suppose it'll take a day or two to get to

Gretna Green, or else to get a license in London. Wickham
says we must see if we "get away clean!"
    Adieu,
    Lydia

Caroline put a hand over her mouth. "She eloped with Mr. Wickham! You were right, Miss Darcy. How did you guess?"

Georgiana pressed her own lips together, feeling sick. "We must... we must tell Mr. Bennet at once. And my brother, of course." She turned away from the mess of Lydia's room.

Caroline followed. "How horrified they will be. I swear there was never anything like it. What a selfish, immoral girl! It will quite ruin the wedding day for the Bennets." Her shock was real, but there was a smug, almost gleeful tone to the last part.

Georgiana turned on her, halfway down the stairs. "Do you think this is unconnected to you and me? She is now a sister-in-law to us both! For shame, Caroline."

John was at the bottom. "I excused the maid about her business, but she is already abuzz with excitement."

Georgiana was still holding the letter. She folded it up and headed for the front door. "Lydia has gone off with Mr. Wickham, an elopement. We must instantly inform her parents. They might yet be able to—to catch up to them." She pulled the door open. "Or perhaps I could send a message but be off instantly?"

Caroline scoffed. "What, go after them yourself? Do not be foolish, Miss Darcy."

John looked dubious. "Certainly not alone."

"No. But consider," Georgiana insisted. "If we go back to Netherfield, which is a quarter of an hour the wrong direction, and then spend some minutes to explain, and more for them to make a decision...We will lose so much time!"

"It would easily cost an hour," John agreed. He pulled a small pocket book out of his coat. "Will you write the note, Miss Darcy?"

She took a pencil from him—how handy artists were!

Lydia left this letter in her room. Mr. Turner is escorting Caroline and myself, as Lydia's sisters, to try and meet them before they continue on. –Georgiana

She folded her note around Lydia's letter and addressed it to, "Mr. & Mrs. Bennet, or Mr. & Mrs. Darcy."

John walked back and rapped on the door. This time it was an older lady, the housekeeper. John gave a half bow. "Could you please send a groom or footman immediately to Netherfield with this note?"

She looked grim. "Miss Lydia has run off?"

"We... hope that whatever has happened can be sorted out at once," John said.

"I understand you. I will keep the servants as quiet as may be." She nodded and withdrew.

Caroline stood tall and haughty. "I am not traveling to Hatfield in a *curricle*."

"We must be off at once," Georgiana said. "Don't you want to catch up to them? If we can find them, we can stop this becoming a scandal."

John offered his hand and Georgiana grasped it to climb into the vehicle.

"I doubt we can stop anything," Caroline said peevishly. "They'll be well away in a chaise and four by the time we get there."

"Oh." Georgiana wanted to stamp her foot. "Wickham is not rich. They probably will take a stagecoach or some such thing, so we might catch them. Please, Miss Bingley."

"It isn't proper for us to go with Mr. Turner such a distance."

"It will be even less proper if I go with him alone." Georgiana's voice rose, "You always say you have my interest at heart. If you ever want me to consider you as a friend, please do me this favor."

Caroline's mouth was a thin line. "Fine." She took Georgiana's hand and squeezed in next to her while John entered from the other side.

"This is most uncomfortable," Caroline added.

Georgiana ignored her. "Do you know the way to Hatfield?" she asked John.

"Yes, that part is easy. Passed through on my way here."

"Good." Georgiana was a little afraid that she was acting foolishly, but the thought of Lydia being duped by Mr. Wickham was disgusting.

John turned the curricle onto the lane.

Being the middle occupant of the small bench seat meant Georgiana was in for an uneasy ride. She braced her feet, having no rail or arm rest to grip at turns or bumps.

John occupied himself with the horses for several moments. Soon they passed through the outskirts of Meryton, and Georgiana thought she recognized the small hostelry where Lizzy's aunt and uncle were staying. There were people on the streets; a boy going on an errand, several ladies walking arm in arm. A man carrying a bundle of rugs. Another man brought in a cart full of early harvest potatoes.

"Need we go straight through the center of town?" Miss Bingley demanded. "It must look so odd."

John apologized. "Perhaps we need not, but I do not know the side lanes and streets and would surely get us lost."

"No one is looking at us," Georgiana said, but this was proven untrue as a covey of young people pointed and waved.

Georgiana waved uncertainly and Caroline gasped, "How dare they?"

"They were probably part of the crowd outside the church," John observed calmly. "They likely assume you are on wedding business."

Caroline muttered angrily under her breath. Even Georgiana was glad when they were out of the main part of the small town. It was one thing to say they must catch Lydia at all costs, another to ride through town to be ogled at in such a way.

"I don't want to be vulgarly inquisitive," John said after a while, "but thinking it over, I cannot quite understand this. I believe your brother said this Mr. Wickham is something of a fortune-hunter. I would not think Miss Lydia Bennet possessed of a fortune."

Caroline snorted. "That she is not."

Georgiana said, "He must...he must think Darcy, or perhaps Mr. Bingley, will settle money on her."

"Why would they do that?" Caroline asked waspishly. "Particularly after this scandal? Most families would disown her."

"Oh dear. What if he doesn't...doesn't intend to marry her at all?" Georgiana asked.

John's hands on the reins were steady and he spurred the two horses to a quicker trot. Georgiana chocked her feet surreptitiously against the front wall of the curricle to withstand the jolting.

"Surely Miss Lydia would not elope under such circumstances," John said.

Georgiana was silent. She did not have it in her to malign the morals of any young lady, even if she were a thousand times worse than Lydia. "She must think he means marriage."

Caroline laughed, rather ugly. "She herself said she wasn't sure whether they went to London or Gretna Green. She doesn't know, or, it seems, care."

A particularly rough bump made Georgiana yelp, as she was jolted forward nearly onto the horse's hindquarters.

"Oh, I apologize, Miss Darcy," John said, "please hold onto my arm, at least."

Georgiana did so as she truly did fear she might be sprung out onto the traces if she wasn't careful. She tried to ignore how snug and comfortable she felt with one arm around his and a firm shoulder to lean on.

She heard Caroline sniff loudly but ignored it. Caroline certainly wasn't offering her own arm.

John could not quite believe the strange adventure they had embarked on, but he was more than willing to do Miss Darcy a service. And if the man who'd thought to trifle with Georgiana for her fortune should need a lesson taught him, John would be too happy to oblige.

He was glad, at any event, that he hadn't left yesterday. Miss Darcy would have needed him.

Hatfield was some eight miles southwest of Meryton, and as he kept the horses at a sharp trot, they made the trip in rather less than an hour.

Meryton was just a small town, but Hatfield was on the Great North Road and was replete with staging inns.

Which of these might be the rendezvous point, assuming their quarry were still here and had not already caught a coach heading north to Scotland or south to London, was anyone's guess.

"This boy who is driving her," John commented, "do you think he is very young? Noticeably young?"

Georgiana frowned. "I do not know for certain. Why?"

"Wondering if they were noticed."

When he passed a likely looking tradesman, John pulled up. He had no intention of burning time scouring the town if he could help it. "Excuse me, sir, which are the best staging inns hereabouts?"

"Oh, ah..." He took in Miss Darcy and Miss Bingley, but didn't seem too concerned. "There's the White Feather and the White Hart, of course. Roebuck Inn, for the mail. Falcombe with Mr. Sopworth."

"That'll do for now. How much further?"

"Half mile. But the mail's already come through. Better try the others."

John nodded his thanks and slapped the reins on the tiring horses.

"Oh, I hope we find them," Georgiana said. "We can't be very much behind, if they were only driving a one-horse gig."

"And we have not seen Mr. Lucas returning either."

Miss Bingley sneered. "Perhaps he has run away as well."

{ 29 }

M R. DARCY WAS TRULY HAPPY, but it was a quiet joy. He would have preferred to leave as soon as the feast was eaten, but he was doing his best to make the party pleasant for Elizabeth, which meant he would not suggest leaving until she did. He was also being as friendly and demonstrative as he knew how. It was uncomfortable, but Lizzy's eyes were sparkling. She positively beamed at him when the crowd demanded a kiss and he smilingly obliged.

Jane and Bingley were going to stay here and begin their journey in the morning, but Darcy had made arrangements for he and Elizabeth to begin their journey tonight. He planned to reach Woburn, if possible, where they could stay with his aunt and uncle on the Fitzwilliam side. They were expecting Elizabeth and him around eight in the evening, if all went well.

When Darcy scanned the room and found Georgiana missing, he frowned. Had *she* grown tired of the party? A quick scan also showed that Mr. Turner was absent, but that Mrs. Annesley was speaking with Mary Bennet, their heads bent over a book. Darcy felt his heartbeat quicken.

He did not think Georgiana would do anything improper, but he had noticed her talking with John less than an hour ago. He had hoped, honestly, that they were saying goodbye. He did not want Georgiana to suffer, but he still hoped that her affection—if any!—would be short-lived. She was young, after all.

Elizabeth, when Georgiana's absence was noted, also looked around the room.

"He is not here," Darcy said.

She grimaced guiltily but didn't deny that had been her first thought. "I think he was set to depart. Perhaps she only walked him down to the front door…"

"Alone?" Mr. Darcy squeezed her shoulder. "Please excuse me for a moment."

Lizzy, taking more time to look over the assembled company, also noticed that Lydia and Miss Bingley were missing, as well as Lizzy's own parents. Heavens, was there a secret meeting taking place? Had the plover eggs gone bad or some such thing?

Feeling reassured about Georgiana, but nervous about the state of the feast, Lizzy slipped out of the ballroom.

Her mother's voice drifted up the stairs from the first floor. "My dear Lydia! But why would she run away? She must know we would not set a bar. Such a charming young man!"

Lizzy's blood ran cold and she flew down the stairs.

The scene which met her eyes was quite awful. Their own manservant, Tom, hovered nearby, hands in his pockets. Her mama held a letter in Lydia's writing, and her father held a scrawl of a note as well. Mr. Darcy's forehead was clenched; his eyes looked quite thunderous.

Her mother thrust the letter into Lizzy's hands. "Oh, this is must unlucky. Why did she not confide in her mama?"

Lizzy read quickly. "Oh, Lydia! How thoughtless! How naïve!" She was torn between a desire to slap her silly sister or to slap the villainous Mr. Wickham.

Her father looked like he was doing a difficult sum. "Wickham? But he was dangling after that Mary King, I am sure. You told me so often enough, Mrs. Bennet."

Her mother cried out at this, though she already seemed to be recovering her spirits. "No! Mary King was whisked away by her guardian months ago, to be sure! It is clearly Lydia he loves, and the thought that he should not trust us quite breaks my heart. They will have so little, poor dears, but how could he think we would reject him for such a reason? Oh, what a handsome couple they will be."

"If he marries her at all," Mr. Bennet said grimly.

"But there is no question—" Mrs. Bennet started.

"This is all my fault." Darcy raised a hand to apologize for interrupting. All eyes turned to him.

Mr. Bennet scoffed. "I fail to see how, sir, unless you knew Mr. Wickham was so base as to run off with a girl of fifteen."

Darcy's mouth was a line. "I'm afraid I knew exactly that. He tried to do so with another young girl, for her fortune, as he probably tried with this poor Mary King. I have no doubt that my… attachment to your family has precipitated this."

"And I knew this about him as well." Elizabeth struck her hand against the balustrade of the stairs. "I could have told her, but it would have involved others… I allowed her to think what she would!"

"The fault is mine. I ought to have made his character known before now."

Mrs. Bennet bristled. "I am afraid, sir, that we already know his character and we hold him in the highest regard. Such a gentlemanly, kind, handsome man!"

Elizabeth winced. "Mama, please hush, you do not know all. He is a gambler, a rake… a complete liar."

Mr. Bennet put a hand to his forehead. "What a catch she has found."

"I must be on my way at once," Mr. Darcy said. "I have already ordered Bingley's phaeton put to. It is quite fast."

Lizzy read the second note, the one from Georgiana, and blanched. "Oh! Georgiana is so good, so generous. She cannot want to run into Wickham. But how she came to be with Mr. Turner and Miss Bingley…"

"That *is* inexplicable," Mr. Darcy agreed dryly.

"I will come with you," Lizzy said. "Only let me get my coat—"

"No." Mr. Darcy drew her aside. "I would accept at once, but think how everyone will talk! You must make excuses for me and hopefully we will be back in an hour or two. More than one reputation is at stake in this matter."

Lizzy at once saw the sense of this and acquiesced. Mr. Darcy kissed her and hurried out the front door to Mr. Bingley's high-sprung phaeton.

AT THE FALCOMBE, THERE WAS NO sign of Lydia or Wickham. Georgiana blushed quite hotly when John asked whether a youth and a young woman in a wagon had stopped there. What a strange look the man gave them. She had not expected a pursuit to be so embarrassing!

At the White Hart, Georgiana released Mr. Turner's arm as her support, so he could direct the horses into the dusty courtyard. Her heart leapt into her mouth as they saw that a stagecoach was in the process of being packed. Many boxes and trunks were already strapped on, and four persons sat in the upper seats. Perhaps…!

In confirmation of her hope, a young man in a wagon was just navigating his way around the stagecoach.

John eyed him. "Mr. Lucas!"

The boy looked up at once. "Yes, sir? I mean, no sir. That's not my name, sir!" He looked quite guilty.

John glared quite sternly. "Tell me the truth."

"I hadn't… she asked me!" he blurted. "I always did like Miss Lydia the best!"

John had pulled to the side so as not to block the entrance to the road, and the young man urged his horse past, red-faced.

Georgiana urged Miss Bingley, "She must be here; do get down!"

"Ouch. Be composed, please, Miss Darcy, you are quite pushing me."

The stagecoach looked to be almost ready to go. Lydia and Wickham might be within already. John's horses were almost nose-to-nose with the stagecoach horses in the crowded yard, and the coachman was yelling at him to "move along there!"

"Don't move them yet," Georgiana said. "Or they will get away!"

John's hands were steady as ever. "I shan't. Only how we are to both block them and get our truant off the coach is beyond me."

Georgiana pushed past Miss Bingley, ignoring her complaints and recommendations, and jumped to the ground. The commotion was awful. The people on top of the coach were also abusing John, shouting at him. Three footmen from the hotel had come out to watch the mess, and Miss Bingley was loudly declaring that she had never been in so vulgar a scene. Without giving herself time to think, Georgiana nipped between the horses around to the stagecoach door and pulled it open.

There were four people within, two older women, Lydia, and Wickham.

Mr. Wickham's face when she jerked the heavy door open was almost hopeful, but when he saw Georgiana, his red mouth fell open in shock. "Good God, Georgiana? Why did Darcy bring *you*?"

Georgiana swallowed, very aware of the others in the coach. "Miss Lydia, I have… urgent news for you. Please do come down at once."

"No. Why should I? I don't know how you found out about this—Kitty, I daresay!—but what I do is my own business."

One of the older ladies gasped.

Georgiana felt like her face would light on fire. "As my sister-in-law, it is also my business and I *must* speak with you. You cannot hope to get to Scotland before you're caught."

The lady who had not gasped, the sterner one, eyed Mr. Wickham. "This is the *London* coach," she said coldly.

Mr. Wickham smoothed his collar collectedly. "Yes, ma'am. The circumstances are not what you think them. This young lady…"

"I suspect the circumstances are exactly what we think them," the stern lady said. "And I, for one, will not ride in a stage with a man of flagrant immorality." Her voice was loud enough for the footmen and the other on-lookers to hear. Wickham was beginning to look flushed.

"I think we had better get off, my dear," he said to Lydia. "Mr. Darcy's rage and resentment are too much to withstand. I was afraid that his ill-will might reach out to snatch this last bit of happiness from us." His words sounded rehearsed and theatrical.

Georgiana frowned. "My brother is not here."

At this, Mr. Wickham finally looked startled, but he was already getting down, so Georgiana stepped back.

When he and Lydia were on the ground, Lydia loudly demanded that her hat boxes be removed. The coachman, already incensed at John's stubbornness, yelled at her to get out of the way.

Lydia stamped her foot. "Don't even think about riding off with my things! That's thievery!"

"Thievery? What about stealing my time, little miss? I ought to turn you over my knee."

Lydia ground her teeth. "I am not a child, sir! I am going to be married and I want my things!"

Miss Bingley was heard to wish that the earth would open and swallow her up. The coachman grumbled angrily about elopements and strumpets, but Lydia's four band-boxes were unearthed. John backed his horses and directed them to the stables on the side of the courtyard.

Lydia sniffed. "Well, you got us off the coach. Shall we just stand here until another comes along?"

Georgiana squared her shoulders. She was significantly taller than Lydia when she tried to be. "Follow me, please."

In the hotel, Miss Darcy pulled together every shred of dignity she possessed, ignored the stares and whispers, and asked for a private parlor. She had no money with her, but the Bennets or her brother would be along soon; someone would pay the expenses. She felt dreadfully foolish and childlike, but if she only knew it, her dignity was quite equal to the occasion. She looked older than her seventeen years, and when she calmly but firmly made her requests, they were instantly obeyed. The servants at the White Hart knew quality when they saw it, even if she had been in the middle of that raucous scene in the yard.

Mr. Wickham and Lydia followed her into the parlor. Lydia, sullen, Mr. Wickham, insolent. Georgiana, whose only plan was to keep them here until someone with more authority arrived, did not like his look.

He had recovered from his surprise at her interference and approached her. "Miss Darcy, it has been too long. I haven't seen you since our time in Ramsgate last summer."

Georgiana narrowed her eyes.

"Don't you have a greeting for an old friend?"

"You are not my friend," Georgiana said.

"Am I not? But how harsh. You used to have kinder words for me, even a kiss on occasion." His look dared her to remember. "But where is your esteemed brother? I rather thought this was the part where he would barge in. That is his role, is it not?"

Lydia wrinkled her nose, confused by his manner of speaking.

{ 227 }

Georgiana shook her head. "Mr. and Mrs. Bennet will be here shortly." She hoped they would.

Lydia understood this all too well. "You already told my parents? I swear, you are as bad as Lizzy! I left a letter for my mama. What right have you to interfere?"

Wickham smiled gently. How did such an evil man look so genteel? "Poor Miss Darcy. You know that our love was doomed, can you blame me for finding love elsewhere?" He touched her cheek. "Your brother forced me to give you up, but at least we can be brother and sister."

Georgiana had not heard the door open behind her, but she saw Wickham look up in annoyance. Then John's fist connected with Wickham's face.

Mr. Wickham did not keel over or pass out, but he stumbled back a few steps and collided with a small table. His hand was pressed over his mouth and when he withdrew it, there was a blood on his fingers.

"What the devil? Who are you?"

{ 31 }

JOHN FLEXED HIS FINGERS. It had been a while since he had a fight. Methodists were not pacifists, like the Friends or Quakers, but they certainly didn't encourage brawling. "My name is Turner; I am Miss Darcy's friend and escort. I take leave to tell you that if you touch her again, you'll regret it."

Lydia rushed to Wickham. "You are hurt!" She turned on John. "How dare you? You have even less to do with us than she does! Has everyone run mad today?"

"It certainly seems so," John agreed.

Caroline entered just behind John and was eyeing the assembly with disgust.

Lydia began to laugh, a touch hysterically. "What is *she* doing here?"

Caroline wrinkled her nose and did an about-face to leave the parlor. "I assure you; I want nothing to do with this. I could use a cup of tea."

"Yes, yes, we all could. Order some for us as well!" Lydia demanded. "I do not know what she is doing here. Poor Wickham! We ought to have gone on at once."

"Miss Lydia," John spoke calmly. "I do not know you well, but I know that you would regret this decision. You're not acquainted with all the details—"

"And you are?" Wickham said, looking suggestively between him and Georgiana.

John flexed his hand again and Wickham stepped back.

Lydia tossed her head. "You're all carrying on as though this was a murder, not an elopement."

"You weren't..." John hesitated. "You weren't even heading to Scotland, but to London. Do you know what that means? That you could not get married because you're underage?"

"Of course, I know that. I am not a child," Lydia repeated. "But we should be married soon! By special license!" she said triumphantly.

"Those are rather expensive," John explained. "And in the meantime, where would you stay?"

"Wickham has rooms already."

"Yes," Wickham agreed dubiously. He dabbed his lip with a handkerchief.

"You can't... stay with him," Georgiana said.

"But we will soon be married," Lydia exclaimed, clearly thinking that made all right. "To be sure, I was a little sad at the wedding today, thinking how I will not get the village cheering for me and the proper feast! Do you not think, Wickham, that perhaps we should explain to my parents? I promise you they like you prodigiously!"

John raised his eyes to the ceiling. "They might like him less after this fiasco."

Wickham glared at him. "Exactly how do you come into this?"

Lydia waved her hand. "Oh, he is only the painter they hired to do Lizzy and Jane's portraits. Miss Darcy fancies him."

The room was very silent, and John forced himself not to look at Georgiana and increase her embarrassment. Mr. Wickham eyed them both. "Does she? A painter? I'm impressed, Mr. Turner, I admit. She's worth thirty thousand pounds, you know. But you *do* know; why else would you pursue her? A nice move getting her to run off after us with you. Perhaps you thought you could turn one elopement into two."

John curled his lip. "There's no point in replying to such fustian as that. You are neither wanted nor needed here, sir. I suggest you take yourself off."

Wickham did indeed look at the door as if pondering whether to go. He straightened his back after a moment and looked the picture of aggrieved nobility. "I would never abandon Lydia in such a heartless way."

"I should think not!" she said.

Georgiana shifted her feet tiredly. If Wickham would not go, they could not very well throw him out. She moved to sit in one of the striped chairs by the tea table. "We may as well sit and have tea. Then we can consider what next to do."

If the Bennets did not soon appear, she must still somehow get back to Netherfield with Lydia this afternoon. Perhaps John could leave his curricle—which barely sat three persons, let alone four!—and hire a larger vehicle to take Lydia back with them.

Wickham laughed, rather unkindly. "You've certainly grown up this year, Georgie."

"I wish I could say the same," Georgiana countered.

Wickham blinked. "And grown claws, I see."

John gave him a level look and Wickham backed down. "Why don't I see what's delaying that tea? I am content to leave my fate in the hands of my *dear* Lydia's parents."

The tea came, along with the return of Miss Bingley, looking decidedly frosty. She did unbend a little to Georgiana, begging that she should drink tea. "For you must be even more exhausted than I! Such generosity of spirit, to go to such trouble for your new family."

Georgiana sighed. Clearly, she was back in Miss Bingley's good graces. That woman would do anything for an invitation to Pemberley.

Lydia was recovering her spirits and chattered while they drank the tea. "Perhaps it is all for the best. It was still hideously interfering of you—busybodies are condemned in church, you know!—but the more I think of it, the more certain I am that we ought to be married in a proper manner. The cake was ever so good, Wickham! The lemonade was only decent, but I declare I drank three cups right off because the service made me thirsty! And we should have red and white roses, rather than the pink Jane and Lizzy used. Perhaps a Christmas wedding?"

Miss Bingley only looked at her contemptuously and urged Georgiana to have a biscuit.

When the maid opened the door, Georgiana assumed it was to clear the tea things, but instead, Darcy strode into the room.

Georgiana's breath left her in a rush; her body nearly sagged in relief.

"I apologize for being late," he said. He walked to stand behind Georgiana and squeezed her shoulder. He greeted the others coolly, "Miss Bingley, your servant, Miss Bennet, Mr. Turner." He did not address Wickham. "I took the liberty of hiring a gig to take us all back to Netherfield."

"Lawd, Mr. Darcy," Lydia said, bemused. "Don't you know this is an elopement? Haven't you anything to say?"

"I have much to say, but my priority is to get all you ladies back to Netherfield without loss of time."

Mr. Wickham stood, nonplussed but seemingly with lines to deliver. "You shall have to deal with me, Mr. Darcy. I won't give Lydia up."

"Spare me your play-acting."

"I will not give up. You cannot always be here to turn me away. You'll be away on a wedding trip, or back at Pemberley. You cannot always—"

"No, I cannot always. Therefore, what? You wish me to pay you to stay away from Miss Lydia? Is that what this farce was for? To force my hand in that way?"

A look of pure hatred flashed over Wickham's face, but it was gone quickly. "Not at all."

"Then what was the plan with this ill-conceived plot? You could have covered your tracks better or waited a few days until I was far away." He turned to Lydia. "I am sorry, but this is not the first time he has fooled a young lady for his own gain."

"You wrong me," Wickham declared. "I am—I am honor-bound to marry Lydia."

"I believe you're going off-script," Mr. Darcy said. "Take care. One afternoon in your company—and not alone, thanks to Georgiana—does not bind her to anything. You might as well get out; you won't get a penny from me."

"Even to save Lydia's reputation? Or if you don't care about that, Miss Darcy's? I have stayed quiet up to now, but if I was to share what I know, she would have a very different season next year."

John tensed. "How dare you?"

Wickham laughed. "How dare I, Mr. *Painter*? How dare *you*? Or does Mr. Darcy even know of your pretensions? I doubt it. The correct Mr. Darcy would not look any more kindly upon *you* than he did upon me."

O N THE CONTRARY, I CONSIDER Mr. Turner a friend," Darcy said. He said it to silence Wickham, but also because it was true. He had not been at all concerned about Georgiana when he knew she was with Mr. Turner. "What next, Wickham? If you carry out your threat to smear my sister's reputation… *either* of my sisters," he added, looking at Lydia, "then I will destroy you. I already discovered you left debts abounding in Meryton. I assume it's the same in Brighton. I can buy them up and send you to debtor's prison. I can inform any regiment of your character and crimes. Have no doubt, I will be believed."

Mr. Wickham still seemed overly confident. "You already cut me off from the living I deserved, will you now make it impossible for me to live another way? No. You don't want Lydia to be ruined or penniless. I think you will help me settle my debts so that I can marry and make an honest woman of her. The great Darcy family with a scandal? I think not."

"Don't be vulgar. This is hardly a scandal," Darcy said sardonically. He was thankful that the culprit had been caught at once. If Lydia had disappeared for days or weeks before they caught up with them, his options would be much fewer. He probably *would* have to set up Wickham with enough money to marry her.

Lydia stuck out her lip. "You have been very harsh to Wickham. And to me! Why shouldn't you help us? I'm sure the money is nothing to you and I *am* your sister now."

She still didn't seem to realize how Wickham was using her; Darcy's opinion of her intelligence sunk even lower. "As my newest, youngest sister-in-law, I am determined to keep you from men such as this. When you're older—"

"I am not a child!" Lydia repeated for the third time. "In fact, I am *with* child."

Darcy froze, as did the others.

Wickham's eyes looked to start out of his head. "Wh— What?"

Lydia put a hand on her stomach. "I am with child. I was not certain in Brighton, but... it is so. We are going to have a baby, Wickham! I hope it is a boy!"

Darcy grabbed Wickham's collar, pulled him out of his seat, and punched him so hard he fell over the edge of the settee and onto the carpet.

"Mr. Turner, would you please escort the ladies out to the taproom? I will be there directly," Darcy said.

"No!" Lydia cried. "You won't hit Wickham anymore! How dare you?"

Darcy rubbed his hand. As much as he wanted to pound Wickham into a pulp, that wasn't the right course. If it was true that Lydia was pregnant, they would have to marry.

Darcy glared at Wickham. The man had made very certain that marriage was the only option, even if the pregnancy itself was a shock to him. Probably he had begun pursuing Lydia when he found out about Darcy's engagement to Lizzy. Lydia was a foolish young girl, but she would not have been Wickham's target if Darcy had not been involved.

Darcy had to right this, as much as possible. He could force Wickham to marry Lydia, but if he gave them nothing to live on, they would only be a drain on the Bennets. Or perhaps Bingley. A new career would be necessary, or at least a new regiment, maybe in the north...

Darcy sighed tiredly. "I will not beat him. Please go with Mr. Turner. I need to speak with Wickham alone."

Wickham stood shakily. His confidence was rattled. He had not intentionally got Lydia with child, but he *had* quite intentionally compromised her, probably to force this exact situation. A situation in which it was by far the best outcome for all if he actually married Lydia; and Darcy had the delightful duty of making it occur.

Georgiana was in a bit of shock as they left the room. Miss Bingley, too, seemed temporarily bereft of speech.

Lydia was crying and declaring that he should not hit Wickham and that she should have a wedding and it was not his fault. Georgiana shushed her as best she could. "You cannot cry in a public room. All will be well, Lydia, all will be well."

But would it? Georgiana knew that early babies did sometimes happen. It was not always cause for a scandal. The girls at school sometimes whispered about such things, but it had seemed distant to Georgiana. Either way, Lydia would need to marry Wickham as soon as possible. Her life would be very difficult otherwise; she would be completely shunned by the society she was born into.

Georgiana wanted to condemn Lydia, but she was forced to recognize that she herself might have ended in the same situation. When Darcy interrupted Georgiana's elopement, Wickham had been banished, but if Georgiana had been…with child, it would not have been so easy!

But she would not have done that. She was *almost* sure she would not have…

But if Georgiana was any wiser than foolish Lydia, it was only because she had been taught better.

They made a small, uncomfortable clump in the tap-room, which was thankfully almost empty in the mid-afternoon. A cool breeze came through the open door, and the smell of beer made Georgiana regret the two pieces of wedding cake she had eaten. Darcy and Wickham finally came out half an hour later.

Mr. Wickham had straightened his clothes, but his lip and eyebrow were split. He was pocketing some money. Lydia went to him and he kissed her cheek. "Good news, pet. I go to obtain the special license tonight, and we will be wed quietly tomorrow."

"Hurray! But quietly? I want all the festivities! I am sure I deserve it as much as Lizzy and Jane."

"There will still be much of the wedding feast left over," Darcy said, like one humoring a child. "I will speak to your uncle about the arrangements."

"Oh, well. I suppose."

Wickham bid her adieu, wincing a little as his lip cracked open again.

When he was gone, Mr. Darcy sighed again. He looked exhausted. Georgiana took his hand. "On your wedding day. I am so sorry."

He shook his head ruefully. "We certainly won't reach Woburn tonight. And I ought to stay and make sure things go smoothly tomorrow."

Caroline tapped her foot. "I, for one, hope to never see Hatfield again. Where is this carriage you ordered, Mr. Darcy?"

She rarely spoke to Darcy that shortly, and it made Georgiana smile in spite of herself. It had been a trying afternoon.

"Dash it all. They must have been walking the horses for an hour," he said.

John cleared his throat. "I need to drive my curricle back to Netherfield. I'm afraid I left my things there in our haste. Then I can be on my way."

Darcy nodded, glancing at John. They were both rubbing their own slightly bruised hands. "Of course. Thank you for your assistance."

"I'm afraid our efforts did not change the outcome."

Darcy acknowledged this with a shrug, leading them out to the stable yard. "Perhaps not the final outcome, but you saved us days or weeks of searching London, which I appreciate. I did get married today."

John smiled. "That you did. I don't believe I yet congratulated you."

"Thank you." Darcy's felt Georgiana's hand on his sleeve, pulling him back for a moment.

She looked at her feet and then back up at his eyes. "Might I ride back with Mr. Turner?"

{ 33 }

DARCY FELT EXHAUSTION CREEPING over him. Not physical, but mental.

He had been, in a sense, beaten by Wickham. Now Georgiana asked this. It was not merely about the ride, he knew that. As rides went, it was acceptable for her to ride for a few miles in an open curricle beside a gentleman, particularly when she would be within hailing distance of Darcy's coach if needed.

But that is not what she was asking. She was asking Darcy to *consider* Mr. Turner. To give, if not his blessing, then something very like it.

It was bold of her. The Georgiana of a year ago would not have done it.

Perhaps she caught him at a weak moment. Perhaps he was softened by having said his own vows that morning. Perhaps the juxtaposition of Lydia and Wickham and what might have been made him thankful that John was quite the opposite of Wickham.

Perhaps he finally recognized that he could not hold her future in his hands forever, and that she could choose far worse than John Turner, middle-class Methodist though he was.

"Yes."

Georgiana's eyes grew huge. "Truly?" she whispered.

"Yes. Well. A *ride,*" Darcy answered. "That is the limit of the current agreement."

"Thank you!" Her eyes welled up.

"You're welcome." He groaned. "As it means that I must drive back with a tearful Miss Lydia and an outraged Miss Bingley, you owe me far more than thanks."

"I know. I owe you everything." Georgiana squeezed his hand.

Darcy squeezed hers. "I love you."

Georgiana waited off to the side while Darcy handed Lydia and Caroline into the carriage. Lydia was not actually tearful at the moment. The news that she would be wed in her own hometown on the morrow was sinking in, and she looked in quite good spirits. Miss Bingley, however, *did* look outraged. Georgiana hoped she wouldn't say many cutting things to Lydia. Perhaps in Mr. Darcy's presence she would not feel comfortable speaking of sensitive topics.

John was talking with the stable hands, thanking them for rubbing down the horses, and paying the stabling charges. He did not notice Georgiana until Darcy's rented carriage pulled away, revealing that she still stood there.

"Miss Darcy," he called, confused. "Shall I flag them down?"

She made her way over to him where he waited. The ostler had poled up his curricle and was now harnessing the horses.

"My brother gave me permission ride back with you," Georgiana explained.

John looked after the carriage for a moment. A flickering smile began to steal across his face. "Did he?"

"Yes."

"Well then, Miss Darcy, please allow me to assist you." He handed her up into the curricle and hurried around to the other side.

The ostler threw him the reins and John tipped his hat. The horses started up and the curricle jolted from side-to-side as they drove from the slightly uneven paving stones of the yard to the smooth road beyond the hotel.

She could almost wish Miss Bingley back; then Georgiana would have a reason to take John's arm again. She was feeling rather shy. It was one thing to ask her brother for this, but quite another to ask a man whether he wanted to marry her.

But Anne did it! Perhaps it was easier for her, however, since she didn't seem to feel every one of Mr. Sutherland's glances like a touch, and his touches like a kiss.

"It's been quite an eventful day and not even half past three," John said, when the silence threatened to become too long.

"Yes." Georgiana rubbed her temples. "I certainly did not think to see Mr. Wickham again for many years. And now he is to be Lydia's husband. I cannot quite believe it."

"Your drawing of him was too generous; it implied qualities where there were none."

Georgiana blushed at the recollection of the sketch he'd seen. "At the time, I saw him differently." She did not want to talk about Mr. Wickham. Oh, this was difficult.

"Having met the man, I can see that he is without decency. I hope you do not still blame yourself for what occurred between you."

"I don't. That is...I thank God that I was protected from worse. Truly, it did not bother me to see him today, not as I thought it would. I pity Lydia for a future with him, but my pain is only for her."

John nodded. "Who a person marries is arguably the most influential decision of their life."

That was an opening, was it not? "That is true. Mr. Turner—John—do you think... Do you also feel that... Oh, this is much harder than Anne made it look!"

The curricle swerved into the weeds at the edge of the road, swaying dangerously close to the ditch. John quickly corrected their course and steadied his hands. He couldn't help but suspect what Georgiana might be trying to say, but was incredulous. It was impossible. Wasn't it?

Did she really have her brother's permission for…whatever this was? Or was there some misunderstanding?

Regardless, John couldn't let her stumble on in uncertainty; that was a gentleman's duty.

John pulled over and transferred the reins to his left hand, taking her hand in his right. "Miss Darcy, are you trying to—to speak of marriage?"

She gripped his hand back. "Yes. Before you leave—"

John cut her off as gently as he could. "Georgiana, I think the world of you; you are kind, beautiful, and wise beyond your years. But I think you also know that we are not…not of the *same* world." He winced at her expression. "It is not a matter of what I would like, but what would be best for you."

She looked up at him, so sweet and trusting. John wanted to stay here forever.

"I do know that," she said, "but I think we agree that *best* is not necessarily what the world deems finest or most sensible. You don't desire the shallow, worldly things of life, so why should I be condemned to them?" She looked down. "Or to marry a man who will expect nothing better of me?"

"Miss Darcy—"

She squeezed his hand. "Now that I have said the word, I must get it all out before I lose my voice. I know that we are different… that I am timid and retiring and you are intimidated by nothing. I know that your family would look askance at me, and vice versa. You want to travel the world, and I would be happy to stay at Pemberley forever. But I think… it would be worth it to be with you. That is, if you felt the same."

"You say all that as if I would be the one sacrificing, but it's…quite the opposite." John brought her hand to his lips and kissed her fingers. "The problem is that I would be reaching too high…"

"Do you not believe that all people are equal before God, as you told Miss Bingley? Take care," she smiled with more confidence, "your veracity is at stake."

"I do." He laughed ruefully. "But, oh, the real world is far from perfect, and in this world, you are the rich, well-educated Miss Darcy."

"Is it the riches that bother you? But only think, we could do all the things you want to do. We could visit the Americas. You could paint anything."

She meant it, clearly. She thought her wealth made her more acceptable, rather than untouchable.

John laughed a little. "But I don't want you for your dowry, I want you for yourself."

"I know. I already have experience with the reverse, perhaps that's why I can tell. I avoided one awful fortune-hunter, please don't make me face a whole season of such men."

John tried once more. "They will not all be like that scoundrel."

"They will not be like you, either."

John cast his eyes up at the fitful clouds in the blue sky. God as his witness, he had tried to be prudent and self-sacrificing.

{ 34 }

WHEN JOHN LOOKED BACK DOWN, Georgiana could see the difference.

"You're right," he said. "I have struggled to keep my distance in vain. When you sat and watched me paint at Rosings, I could barely keep my hands steady. When you were sick, I wanted to comfort you." He raised his hand and stroked her cheek. "I want to be the man who sits next to you while you play. I want to turn the pages. Request my favorite songs. Learn yours. I want to be the man who makes you completely forget that cad. I want to be the man who loves you. Who grows old with you."

His hand cupped her cheek and Georgiana put hers over it.

John took a shuddering breath. "If by some miracle your brother does not come to his senses and refuse my suit, will you marry me?"

"Yes," Georgiana whispered. "Yes, I will."

John leaned toward her, but the crack of a whip and rattling of wheels meant someone was coming up behind them.

The other driver, who looked to be a prosperous farmer, called out as he came abreast of them. "Ho! Trouble there? Might I be of service, sir?"

"No, thank you," John said. "We only paused to...discuss the route. No trouble."

"The route? Are you lost?"

"We were," John said, smiling recklessly at Georgiana, "but I think we are on the right path now."

He slapped the reins and the horses started again, pulling ahead of the wagon which was slower than their vehicle.

"Good day!" John added.

Georgiana straightened her bonnet. "I daresay he will stay behind us all the way to Meryton."

"That would be unfortunate," John agreed. "Because I very much want to kiss you and I cannot very well do it with him just behind us."

Georgiana blushed.

John continued, "But perhaps it's just as well. I cannot quite believe that your brother—he is your guardian, yes?—would ever agree."

"My brother and my cousin, Colonel Fitzwilliam, share guardianship, but the Colonel will follow my brother's lead."

"Ah." John held out his elbow. "Will you at least take my arm, madam? I think we can do so much without flaunting propriety."

Georgiana wrapped her hand around his arm, sliding closer on the seat. "I could drive this way forever."

Unfortunately, the drive had to come to an end. They arrived within five minutes of Darcy's party, who were still in the vestibule.

It looked as if the wedding feast must be done. Of the line of carriages that had arrived at Netherfield earlier, now only two carriages still sat near the house. The crowd of grooms who'd lounged near the stables drinking home-brewed out of tankards had also disappeared. The celebration was over.

Georgiana entered the house on John's arm, but no one noticed.

Lydia had fully recovered her spirits and was telling Lizzy with much excitement that she was to be married to-morrow.

Mr. and Mrs. Bennet were coming more slowly down the stairs; Lizzy had run down ahead of them. Caroline was nowhere to be seen.

"And so, Darcy and Wickham made the arrangements and it is settled!" Lydia crowed. "Wickham will be back in the morning with a special license!"

Mrs. Bennet clasped her hands at her bosom as she reached the bottom step. "A special license! Oh, my darling Lydia! How romantic."

Mr. Bennet directed a questioning look at Mr. Darcy. "Tomorrow?"

Darcy inclined his head. "It seemed best to me. You will wish to speak with Lydia privately—"

"Tomorrow?" Mrs. Bennet shook her head. "I can never be ready! The day after a double wedding! No, at least a week, I insist."

Lizzy looked grave. "He is...willing to marry?"

Darcy flexed his hand. "He is. I settled it as best I could. He has left his regiment in some distress, but I think I might be able to get him a new commission with a general who does not know him. Perhaps in the north."

"The north?" Mrs. Bennet repeated blankly, embracing Lydia. "You are already taking Lizzy far from home, shall you rob me of another daughter, too?"

Mr. Darcy opened his mouth and shut it firmly.

Lizzy put her hand on his arm. "Let us go into the library, or somewhere less public, and hear the rest."

"Oh, la, there are no servants present." Lydia waved a hand. "The thing is that Mr. Wickham and I knew we would marry soon, but it happens that I am increasing, so perhaps it ought to be as soon as possible. You know how people do count the months, Mama."

The little room off the entryway was suddenly as silent as the celebration had been noisy.

Even Mrs. Bennet, who was still fondly hanging on her youngest daughter, stepped back and pressed a hand to her bosom. "Oh, Lydia."

Lizzy looked as if she might cry. Mr. Bennet was sternly angry.

Mr. Bennet flicked a look at John and snapped at Lydia, "A fine way to make such an announcement. Please excuse us, sir."

John bowed and released Georgiana's hand with a squeeze, removing himself from the room.

"Oh, he knows already," Lydia said. "He brought Miss Darcy to spoil my fun, but I don't hold it against either of them, for I admit that it is much more the thing to be married by special license than over the border."

"But to such a man," Lizzy said slowly. "Lydia, do you solemnly wish to marry him? He ought not to have... Lydia, he compromised you. If you do not wish to marry him, perhaps there is another way..."

Lydia laughed. "But we knew we should be married soon! Such a wonderful, handsome officer! As if I should not wish to marry him! Mama understands, I am sure."

"I do, my dear, I do. It is not quite...but my daughter, Mrs. Wickham! And—and—" she cupped Lydia's face, "I will be a grandmother! Oh, Lydia, a baby! You were all the most delightful infants, except for Mary, and at times Kitty, but I daresay your child shall not be so difficult or sickly. In fact, even Jane was not so beautiful and good-humored that first year, but you yourself were such a bouncing, strong-willed infant! How I laughed at your tantrums and stubborn demands. Oh, it is beyond anything!"

Mr. Bennet cleared his throat, looking tired. "I must speak to Mr. Darcy alone. Please excuse us from any more of this...this nonsense."

Neither Lydia nor Mrs. Bennet looked perturbed at this blighting comment, though Georgiana instinctively shrunk a bit.

Darcy led Mr. Bennet to the library where they could be private. The older man was faintly gray around the mouth. He sat heavily in one of the armchairs near the empty fireplace.

He'd aged twenty years in a day. "I assume you gave Wickham the money for the special license."

"Yes, sir."

"What are the odds he'll disappear with the money and never show his face in Hertfordshire again?"

"I believe he will come tomorrow," Darcy said uncomfortably. He sat, wishing he'd changed out of his wedding finery and could shove his hands in the pockets of his riding breeches.

"If you think that," Mr. Bennet said shrewdly, "you must have promised him a fair sum for marrying her. He'd be a fool to take less than ten thousand."

"Not quite that."

"Well, sir? At what price am I dipped for my daughter's honor?"

Darcy leaned back in his chair, crossing one foot over the other. "You are not. As your son-in-law, I hope you consider me a member of your family. As such, please allow me to assist in this matter."

"Yes, a part of my family for nearly four hours now," Mr. Bennet said dryly.

Darcy leaned forward again. "Even if I was not yet married to Elizabeth—even if she would not have me—I would never have been able to see her or her family suffer without wishing to mitigate it. Please allow me the honor of doing her this service. Also, it is at least partly my fault that he imposed on the innocent community of Meryton and made a good impression on Lydia."

"Yes, you said that before, but I have been remiss with her. Lizzy even warned me not to let her go to Brighton! No, I let Lydia fill her empty head with officers and foolishness and took no great care that better furniture should be installed there."

Darcy was rather in agreement with this—at least that Mr. Bennet could have taken a more active role in raising his daughters to be educated and sensible. But...

"I feel I ought to tell you that the young woman I mentioned before, the one he convinced to elope, was Georgiana. I visited unexpectedly and she told me the whole affair before it could be executed, but you may draw what comfort you will from the fact that your daughter is not the first to have her sense overridden."

Mr. Bennet put a hand over his eyes. "What a charming son-in-law. Perhaps presently that will comfort me. In fact, it probably will, for I am indolent and dislike unpleasant chores. At the moment, I can only thank you and for once own how at fault I have been. Please leave me for now. I must prepare myself for tomorrow."

Darcy rose, bowed, and withdrew. Let the older man have some time alone. Perhaps his soul-searching would benefit Mary and Kitty.

Sighing, Darcy went to John's room and knocked.

{ 35 }

THERE WAS NO ANSWER. Darcy took himself to the rear parlor, which had been the painting room, and there he found the painter.

The room was empty of art paraphernalia, and looked what it had once been: a rather sad, neglected little room. Mr. Turner was seated by the window with a book open in his lap.

"Good Lord," said Darcy, "are you reading a Bible?"

John looked up. "Yes. Is that a problem?"

Darcy came in and shut the door behind him for privacy. "Not at all, but if you were a manipulative man, I would say you were playing the role rather over-the-top."

John closed the book. "Well, I am facing a decision that will affect my obedience and devotion to God; it seemed fitting to consult Him."

"Would that not be prayer?"

"I prefer to do both. Prayer is man speaking to God, but how will God answer if not through his spoken Word?"

"Yes. I've heard the Wesleyans are quite mad after the Scriptures." Darcy dropped tiredly into the one comfortable chair in the room.

"And while I would enjoy trying to convince you of it, that is not why we need to speak," John said.

"Indeed not. Well, sir?" Darcy was not going to say it for him.

John was already sitting up straight, but he adjusted himself to face Darcy. "I would like to request your sister's hand. I am more than aware that in the world's eyes she can do far better, but I love her very much."

"On my wedding day, I can hardly dispute about love," Darcy said ruefully. "But it still feels wrong to consider your suit. As a man of serious morals, can you understand my dilemma? You seem a solid sort of man but marrying you will mean...a harder life for her. I don't mean materially."

"Yes. I don't deny it; your society will look askance at her for marrying someone little better than a tradesman. It is unconventional at best. But, as Georgiana herself persuaded me earlier today, she *wants* something different. I want to be the best man that I can before God, and I believe she wants the same for herself. And for what it's worth, I will always take care of her; I will be considerate, compassionate, and faithful."

Darcy nodded. "Sadly, that is not true of many men in society."

"Exactly. She might face adversity in her life, but not from me."

"Speaking of adversity, you are aware that the man you met today is the one who convinced Georgiana to run away with him?"

"Yes, she told me about it some time ago."

"Her position was not quite the same as Lydia's; Georgiana believed Wickham to be one of her oldest friends, but the similarities are there. Does that matter to you?"

"No," John said plainly.

"Very well. You spoke to her this afternoon?" Darcy inquired on a lighter note.

"Yes. Er, I could almost say she spoke to me."

Darcy's brow furrowed. "I must say, you don't seem the sort I would expect her to fancy herself in love with."

John smiled. "I know. I'm not a tall, handsome fellow, the kind ladies prefer. Nor have I flirted with her or flattered her. Please believe that if I thought she was just suffering an infatuation, I would be the first to walk away."

"You nearly did walk away, did you not? It was Georgiana who precipitated this." Darcy shook his head. "It is not like her."

John agreed. "Even on my shorter acquaintance, I can see her confidence is unusual. Perhaps that is why I am now convinced she is in earnest."

"And if I said you needed to wait until her coming-out? Or until her majority? That would be over three years."

John didn't relish the idea of so many years passing. What if Miss Darcy forgot about him? But as soon as he thought that, he realized it was all the more reason to wait. "I would, of course, respect that decision. She is young and if you think she ought to wait, if you think she might change her mind, you definitely ought to make such a stipulation."

Darcy sighed. "You are imminently reasonable, Mr. Turner. It is frustrating. If you were to show some immaturity or meanness of character, I would feel justified in sending you packing."

"I apologize?"

Darcy laughed and sighed. "I will not make either of you wait that long. I suspect Elizabeth would have something to say about it."

"Are you...agreeing? Does this mean that we may be formally engaged?"

"I suppose so, but I would like to wait a few months to make an announcement. I fear there would be even more gossip if the hasty wedding tomorrow is followed by a hasty announcement of Georgiana's engagement."

"Oh. That is a good point."

"I was already planning to host a Christmas gathering at Pemberley this year. What if we say that you and Georgiana may be engaged and correspond in the interim, but the official announcement to friends and family will be made at that time? You would join us for Christmas, of course."

"I think that's an excellent idea. She will have time to think over the ramifications of this."

"But you do not think she will change her mind, do you?" Darcy asked.

"Will I sound a coxcomb if I say no? But my certainty is not based on my qualities, but a trust that she knows her own mind."

Darcy rose to his feet. "Very well. My father and mother would be shocked at this day's work from start to finish, but Georgiana recently reminded me that we cannot make decisions on memory and nostalgia alone. What's more, I think my mother would have liked you."

"Thank you, sir." John shook his hand, not quite believing what had transpired.

"You're welcome." Darcy rubbed his temple with his other hand. "Why don't you accompany me to the study? You might drink water, but I desperately need a scotch."

{ Epilogue }

MARTHA, RUTHIE, AND SILAS TURNER pressed close to the cold glass of their school room window, peering down at the carriage that had drawn up below. The town of Plympton was dusted with snow, and it looked as if the carriage had been powdered with sugar.

Silas had established already that the snow was too dry to form into snowballs, which he suspected was due to the height and composition of the clouds. Silas had a scientific mind and was the sort of boy who *could* memorize Latin declensions in his sleep, but much preferred to investigate the properties of the environment.

He had come in half an hour past with red, stinging hands, having done experiments and also having enjoyed the unusual snowfall for all it was worth. Science aside, more than one handful made its way into his sisters' collars. They had screamed and flung snow at him as well, scraping it off the paving stones that led to the front door, the lintels of the windows, and anywhere else it stuck.

The snow was a welcome break from lessons in mathematics, which were twelve-year-old Silas's current bane. His books were open on the desk by the door, while the girls' lexicons were spread on the table in the middle of the room. The girls didn't spend as much time in the schoolroom as they used to, often helping their mother instead, but their father still encouraged them to keep up their Greek.

"It is not so fine a carriage," Silas said, disappointed. His snub nose was flattened against the pane. "I thought Jack was marrying a great swell."

"It is not *her* carriage," Martha corrected him. "Since Jack is bringing her to visit, he would be the one to hire one."

The carriage door opened and their oldest brother, John, or Jack as they called him, sprang out. They couldn't see his face for his hat, but they could see the lady he handed out next.

"Is she not so tall and elegant?" Martha breathed.

Silas sniffed. It had not been much of an event for him when Maisie and Sally wed. First of all, they both still lived in the village, and second of all, losing two sisters, both of whom ordered him about as if they were second mothers, was not a great loss. When his middle brother, Peter, had joined the regulars, that had been more difficult. And now

Jack, who Silas rather idolized, was also to start a new part of his life.

Of course, Jack had not lived at home in Plympton for years, but when he did come home, he was immediately Silas's best friend again. They always shared the boys' room, lying on the narrow beds that had been shoved into the attic space. They carried up a warming pan and stayed up late talking about Jack's work and Silas's friends and hobbies.

Now, Jack was bringing a fiancée. Silas couldn't see much of the lady as they walked quickly to the front door, but he caught a look Jack threw up at their window, though the angle wouldn't allow them to be seen.

Ruthie ran to the door, but Martha hissed at her. "No, we must wait for Mama to call us down."

"I was only going to crack it open," Ruthie said with injured dignity. She did so. All three came and stood near.

They could hear the muffled sound of introductions— their father had stayed at home for this visit—and the familiar sound of Jack's voice.

They did not have to wait long before they heard footsteps taking the stairs. The door was thrown wide and Jack laughed.

"You are all standing like statues. Hello, Si." He hugged his brother, then his sisters. "Ruthie, Martha. Come down and meet Georgiana."

Mrs. Turner, John's mother, was torn between pride that her son made such a brilliant match, and a deep distrust of all things fashionable and frivolous—a category she believed most of the upper class belonged in. If Georgiana had been a great beauty, particularly a blonde beauty—for prejudice is seldom logical—Mrs. Turner might have taken years to warm up to her. But as it was… Mrs. Turner saw a rather common-place girl with brown hair and eyes, unremarkable except for being rather tall and having an air of calm dignity. She was not plain; she was not beautiful.

Her pelisse was dark green and fine but not at all flashy. Her hair was not in riotous curls, a la Sappho, but smooth, parted in the middle, and confined.

Better than any of this—for despite her prejudices and preferences, Mrs. Turner was a perceptive woman—there was a look in Georgiana's eyes that reassured her. This girl would not try to turn John into something he was not.

Mrs. Turner went to retrieve the tea things.

Mr. John Turner, the elder, was glad Jack was marrying. High time. Nice young girl. Already attending class meetings in her hometown, apparently. Perhaps he could interest her in Greek.

Silas bowed after Ruthie and Martha gave their curtseys. He did not see what all the fuss was about. Miss Darcy looked very normal. She was prettier than Sally and Ruthie, but not as pretty as Maisie and Martha, he thought critically.

They sat for tea; *that* at least was special. Silas was not so scientific as to spurn treats of the flesh. His mother brought out warm scones and biscuits, cooked for the occasion, and cold clotted cream which had been sitting on the outer sill of the kitchen window all morning.

"These are delicious," Miss Darcy said. "Thank you."

"Martha made them," Silas said, wanting to give his sister her due. "She is good at baking. Ruthie is better at lessons, though." Both sisters stared at him as if he'd sneezed all over the table. Silas took another scone.

"What are you good at?" Miss Darcy asked. Like a sensible person.

"Latin," he sighed. "But I do not like it. I would like to be a chemist. What are you good at?"

Ruthie shushed him.

"No, it's fine," Miss Darcy said. "I love to play the pianoforte. I like to sketch. I am afraid my current skills are not particularly useful."

Martha wished to ask whether Miss Darcy had fallen in love with Jack over their shared love of art and music. But was that a question one could ask a newly met, almost-sister-in-law? She feared not.

Georgiana could not think what to say after the weather and the deliciousness of the food had played out.

Like her brother, Georgiana became unfortunately formal when she was nervous. With all the will in the world to build a friendship with John's family, she and they may not have gotten beyond a stiff goodwill if it wasn't for the cat.

A handsome black and white cat sauntered into the room from the direction of the kitchen. It had been aware of the cream all morning and was now coming to see where it had gone.

"Oh, what a beautiful animal," Georgiana said. "I have never owned a cat, but always wished to."

The elder Mr. Turner bobbed his head. "Quite what I say. Excellent beasts; they keep the mice away from the house and the rice away from the mouse." He laughed at his own rhyme and his children smiled indulgently.

"What's his name?" Georgiana asked.

"It's a she, Maggie. She's a magpie, you see," Mrs. Turner answered with both fondness and embarrassment in her voice. In her secret soul, she feared perhaps her love of the cat was not scripturally sound. "Normally we would not have her indoors with a guest here, but with the snow it seemed harsh to put her out."

"No, of course not." Georgiana leaned down to offer her fingers to the cat who obligingly sniffed and allowed Georgiana to stroke her back. "She's so soft."

"Yes," Mrs. Turner said, "but do be careful, she likes to play."

A True Likeness

That was when things began to go wrong. For the cat *was* playful; it turned and batted at Georgiana's hand. She would not have minded this, but one of the cat's claws snagged the simple engagement ring John had given her. The cat jerked her paw away, scratching Georgiana rather sharply. Georgiana's tea, held properly in her lap, was upset. Tea splashed on her pelisse and on the cat.

With a startled hiss, the cat streaked away.

"Oh, I am sorry," both Georgiana and Mrs. Turner said.

But the front door, visible just through the vestibule, opened at the same time, letting in a blast of cold air. Several people, bundled to the eyes and slightly snowy, piled into the entryway. A rather broad young lady who looked significantly like John called, "Mama, we are sorry to be late—"

But the cat, seeing the open door, darted through their feet and tripped the lady.

Clutching at her husband, Maisie went down in a tangle of boots and scarves.

Silas hopped up and dashed forward to retrieve the cat. Mrs. Turner alternated between apologies and demands that Silas shut the front door before all the heat in the house was gone.

Maisie was laughing loudly as her husband helped her to her feet; the clean floor was becoming slippery with melted snow.

Martha was frozen. Ruthie loudly pointed out that Sally, James, and Baby Robert were just coming up the walk as well, so it was no point to shut the door yet.

The cat had escaped out the front door, but stopped in the snow, shaking each paw in turn with disgust.

Silas grabbed her around the middle, and he, Sally, James, and the baby entered together, finally shutting the door.

The baby began crying and reaching for the cat, which slunk under the Christmas tree to lick its wet fur. Maisie and Sally commiserated on the ice that was forming on the roads.

John greeted his brothers-in-law, whom he'd not seen in some time, and Mrs. Turner sat down limply in her chair.

"I apologize, Miss Darcy, it is not always so chaotic here."

Georgiana, who was quite enjoying the family scene—and much more comfortable now that the entire attention of the family was not on her—refreshed Mrs. Turner's tea. "Have another cup, ma'am, I'm sure you deserve it after preparing all morning. How old is your grandbaby? Is he talking yet?"

Georgiana poured out tea for the newcomers, who gladly took up the warm cups in their hands as they greeted her with friendly exclamations. They did not even sit, but stood in groups talking, the men still in the entryway, the ladies in the sitting room. It was casual and loud but full of affection.

Maisie cupped Georgiana's hands with her own, leaning forward to kiss her cheek. "I am so happy for Jack. He's the best of big brothers." She called to him, "Jack! I always knew you would flatter a portrait-sitter too much one of these days! Did I not say so?"

John laughed. "I do not flatter unless I have to, I've told you."

Maisie looked at Georgiana. "But he did paint you?"

"Yes." Georgiana smiled.

"How romantic." Martha sighed. She had retrieved the baby and was holding him on one hip, giving him bits of scone.

"Romantic?" Georgiana glanced at John, eyes twinkling. "I suppose. But it is no easy thing to maintain composure when you are falling in love with a man and must sit and look at him all morning."

Maisie squealed. "I can just imagine! When he wrote to me of your engagement, I was glad for him, but now that I have met you, I am doubly so."

"Thank you."

"Of course! Now, Georgiana—do you go by Georgiana, by the by? We are rather informal, you see. Our Christian names are John, Sarah, Mary, Peter, Martha, Ruth, and Silas," she rattled them off quickly, "but as you see, we go by Jack, Sally, Maisie, and so on."

"Except me," Martha put in. "They tried to call me Mattie, but I told them I am too old for that."

"Martha is such a pretty name. I never had a nickname," Georgiana answered. "But I am not opposed to it. I did not know John was called Jack."

"Oh yes, in order not to be confused with Father!"

The baby boy suddenly lunged nearly out of Martha's arms. "Kitty!"

The cat had come out while she was not being observed and coolly helped herself to the cream on the table.

"Oh, drat that cat!" Mrs. Turner said, whisking the cream away from the animal. "I am so embarrassed, Miss Darcy. You must think we live in Bedlam."

"No, she is fine, Mama," Maisie said. "Look how her eyes smile; she does not mind us. Not like that odiously fine girl Peter brought home to visit! And you cannot keep calling her Miss Darcy, she will soon be part of the family."

Georgiana tentatively scooped the cat off the table and found her content and purring after her treat. She brought the cat close for Baby Robert to pet. "I am very happy to be part of your family. Is your own family growing? Er...I apologize if I should not ask..." Georgiana suddenly feared this charming family had loosened her tongue too much, but Maisie laughed.

"Yes, I am as wide as the doorway, am I not? Baby Robert shall have a cousin before long, Lord willing."

"Does Robert not have a nickname?" Georgiana asked.

Ruthie, who had come to take a second biscuit, leaned in. "James is more formal than we are. Si used to call him

Rob or Bobby, and James threatened to tan his backside if he persisted."

Maisie laughed. Mrs. Turner shook her head. "Silas would not be injured by an extra switching or two."

The remainder of the pleasant afternoon passed too quickly for Georgiana. She was glad that they had planned to stay the night with John's family, since the carriage-ride back to Pemberley was nearly five hours.

"We hope you will not mind sleeping in Martha and Ruthie's room," Mrs. Turner said, with a slight return of her former stiffness.

"I was delighted when John told me the arrangements. I have never had sisters, you know."

The Turners did not dress for dinner, which felt slightly odd to Georgiana, but she had to admit it was simpler. When it was time for bed, after a round of goodbyes to the couples who lived in town, she found her bag had been laid on the bed that "used to be Sally's."

She used the basin on the small dresser to wash her face, followed by Martha and Ruthie, who dumped the used water into the pail and poured fresh water from a pitcher.

"This is fun," Ruthie said. "I hope you will come again next month for Christmas."

"I am hoping that you will visit us for Christmas at Pemberley," Georgiana said, deciding on the spot. Christmas was when her engagement would be an-nounced, after all. "Every year our housekeeper has boughs of holly, mistletoe, ribbons, and bells hung throughout the house for the public days; I know you would enjoy it."

Ruthie looked impressed. "Do people travel to see your house?"

"Some do, I suppose. Many are tenants or local towns-people…"

Martha's eyes shone. "I would love to see your home, Miss Darcy."

"Ruthie, Martha, you can call me—" she almost said *Georgiana* but at the last moment, she switched. "Please call me Anna."

Ruthie grinned. "Like the Empress of Russia! You *are* very stately."

Georgiana dropped a curtsey. "Thank you. But the empress is getting cold and must retire."

She snuggled down into the bed, her feet finding the hot spots from the old-fashioned warming pan they'd used a few moments ago. Silas had come to help them with it, before taking the warming pan to his and John's attic room.

"Goodnight, Anna," Ruthie and Martha said.

"Goodnight." Georgiana fell asleep feeling that she had truly entered another life now, but one that bore a truer likeness to her soul than the one she had given up.

The End

Keep reading with *A Gentle Touch,*

Book 3 of An Austen Ensemble

A
NNE DE BOURGH IS NOW Anne Sutherland, wife and mistress of Middlefinch, a large estate in the south of England.

She is satisfied to have done so well for herself, and yet, she finds living with her husband and her new family rather more alarming than she expected.

Her new husband is so informal—he gives his son rides on his shoulders, wrestles with the dogs, and concerns himself with all manner of hands-on farming duties.

His mother is an outdoorswoman, happier in the stables and kennels than anywhere else. She is only too happy to relinquish the duties of mistress to inexperienced Anne.

And Mr. Sutherland's daft old uncle leads his own strange life on the third floor, emerging only to make disconcerting exclamations.

Even if she can grow accustomed to all this, there is still the matter of learning what to do with the kindness and affection of her husband.

Anne has learned friendship; can she learn love?

Author's Note

THANK YOU FOR READING! I did not intend to write a trilogy when I began *A Lively Companion*, but I couldn't bear to stop when clearly Georgiana was about to be packed off to stay with Lady Catherine!

Mr. Turner was inspired by John Wesley Jarvis, a real regency painter—but in name only. As soon as I saw his name a whole character sprang fully to mind—Methodist, middle class, strong but not flashy, and above all, self-controlled.

I am not a Methodist, so I apologize if I mischaracterized anything in regard to the early days of that denomination. I thoroughly enjoyed the research, and, much like Georgiana, quite liked the mindset of the "methodical," Methodists.

I am sure that she and John would have their share of culture shock during the course of their marriage, but I am confident they would find their way.

But then, what of Anne de Bourgh? I found myself unexpectedly fond of forthright Mr. Sutherland, who was originally a bit of a villain until I realized that he was not at fault for the situation with Georgiana. I very much wanted to examine Anne's journey as she learns to lead a richer emotional life as a wife and stepmother. Don't miss the end of the story as our favorites attend a christening, the Turners visit Pemberley for Christmas, and Anne navigates her first year of marriage.

If you need more to read after An Austen Ensemble, you might also enjoy *Pride & Prejudice & Passports*, my modern retelling of Pride and Prejudice, or *The Rise and Fall of Jane*, my sci-fi/paranormal retelling of Jane Eyre.

Thanks again for joining me!

Corrie Garrett

Who am I? I'm an indie writer and homeschool mom in Southern California. I enjoy writing both romance and science fiction with angst, humor, and happy endings.

Find me on Facebook at Corrie Garrett, Author.
Or on my website: www.corriegarrett.wordpress.com

Made in the USA
Columbia, SC
13 April 2021

36122676R00171